THE Monster IN HIM

THE *Monster* IN HIM

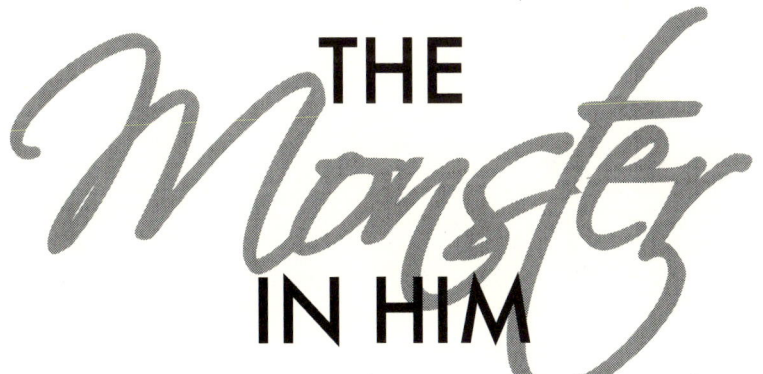

One Woman's Story of Surviving Domestic Abuse

A memoir by
Desiree Joy Arias

Copyright © 2022 by Desiree Joy Arias
All rights reserved. This book or any portion thereof may not be reproduced or used in any manner whatsoever without the express written permission of the publisher except for the use of brief quotations in a book review.

Edited by Sandra Wissinger
Formatted by Alejandro Martin

For more info email arias.desiree@hotmail.ca

DEDICATION

I dedicate this book to anyone, man or woman, who has ever been in an abusive relationship. I dedicate this book to those who are still in an abusive relationship, to those who still have hope and to those who feel as though hope and escape are only words from children's books. I also want to dedicate this novel to those unfortunate women who have left this world at the hands of their abusers.

I would also like to express gratitude for the friends and the families of victims who stuck by them through all the tough times, no matter how rocky it got. I understand it is a difficult task and the world needs more people with this kind of strength and love.

Contents

Preface   1

Introduction   7

Chapter 1   13
Sweet, Innocent, Naive

Chapter 2   21
This Could Be Love

Chapter 3   33
A Different Side Emerges

Chapter 4   45
Losing Control

Chapter 5   53
Struggling to Be Independent

Chapter 6   69
An Unkind Hand

Chapter 7   83
Manipulated and Alone

Chapter 8   97
Fighting for Control

Chapter 9   111
From Bad to Worse

Chapter 10   127
The Promise Ring

Chapter 11   141
The Party

Chapter 12   153
My Final Breath

Chapter 13   173
The Final Blow

Chapter 14   195
Escape

Epilogue   211

Red Flags   217

PREFACE

My story begins the way many others do. I was young, dumb and I thought I was head over heels in love. At the age of fifteen, you want to believe in love. You have faith that someone who says they love you would do anything for you. You believe this person will let no harm come to you, protect you in every way they can and love you no matter what. I'm horribly saddened to have learnt the hard way that this is not always true, especially at an age when no one really knows what love is or what it means to love someone.

THE Monster IN HIM

I'm sad to tell you that I have had a man—well, a boy—repeatedly tell me how much he loved me as he literally sat on my already fractured ribs. Unfortunately, there are many stories out there like mine—and some are even worse. However, women are afraid—petrified, in fact—to talk about their experiences and the horrors they have lived through.

Even though there is help out there, talking about physically abusive relationships is still taboo. No one really talks about it. I am referring to a real conversation. Even among people in these types of relationships, it is not discussed. It may be obvious what is happening, but it is not acknowledged. It is like the use of Voldemort's name in Harry Potter; it is never mentioned—forbidden to speak of. If an incident is noticed, it is quickly forgotten about.

Those of us who are not scared anymore and want to open up and talk about our experiences are faced with a massive stone wall. The people who make up this wall—people who love us, such as family and friends or spouses and partners—though they care for us deeply, do not want to hear the gruesome, graphic stories of the horrible things that a person they love has endured.

When my best friend stopped talking to me after many encounters with my situation—although I'm sure she thought she was doing the right thing at the time for herself and for me—it only pushed me further down the rabbit hole, further into my quiet shell of a life and further into the arms of my abuser. I have to remind myself often that people are afraid of what they do not understand, and though this may be true, it is not an excuse to turn a blind eye.

To overcome their struggles, survivors of abuse want nothing more than to be listened to. To anyone out there who has a friend or family member who is in an abusive relationship: I know that it's very hard to watch someone you deeply care for go down that path and retreat from the world, but though they may not reach out to you, it doesn't mean they don't need you anymore. They are just waiting to come up for air and see the light, hoping that someone will be there. So, for anyone out there who knows someone in need, you don't need to babysit them, but if you really care, wait by the exit sign. When they are ready, they will come to you. I can guarantee you they will be eternally grateful you didn't abandon them.

The stone wall is also built of skeptics and those who criticize victims of abuse. What I've most encountered when the subject is brought up is dismissiveness by a singleminded person who thinks they know how others should live their lives. They simply say, "Why didn't she just leave?"

Well, if only it was that easy. If only the woman could say "*I'm done*," reach for the doorknob, turn it without hesitation, open it to a beautiful garden and just walk out into a bright, sunny world. If only she could hear the door close quietly behind her as she walked down the road, unharmed and able to start a new life without ever hearing from her abuser again. I'm sure that for the people who tried to do it that way—just walking out—it didn't work out the way they thought or hoped it would.

The thing people don't understand is that the abuser always has ways of manipulating their victim and isolating them until they feel as though life is better with the abuser than without them, no matter how silly it sounds to some. It's like you're a fish on a hook and your abuser is holding the line. They let you out a bit and give you some slack, only to drag you back in whenever they so choose. At first, you resist. But then, they pull. You struggle harder but eventually get tired—too tired to fight and the waves of the world push you back and forth.

This person now feels like your life raft, your only chance of survival, as they are now the only thing keeping you from getting completely lost in the expanse. So, you stop fighting. You give in to the person holding the fishing line. Why? Because you know you're caught and after all you've fought, you feel depleted. You no longer have a choice. They drag you out of the water and onto their boat—and once you are on their boat, it's hell. And trying to escape hell is a treacherous feat as the vicious cycle begins again.

It's been about nine years now. Though my physical scars are long gone, my emotional scars remain. Insecurities I've acquired are raw and open to the world. They've become a part of who I am, and it's a struggle. Every day I get a little stronger, but the remnants of what happened are always with me in the back of my mind. It has taken me a long time, but now I want to tell my story. Anytime I try to, however, I feel as though it falls on deaf ears.

I feel misunderstood at times because no one really knows what has happened to me. Up until now, I've kept quiet about the whole thing because of that massive wall. I've spared those around me the grief, but inside I am struggling. I've seen many therapists, but I still feel very alone. I'm hoping to connect with others who might understand and need some assurance.

I am opening the floodgates. I am lifting the gag order on domestic violence in hopes of helping people understand what it means to be in an abusive relationship. I've decided to write this book so that I and others who know what it feels like can heal through communication, validation and understanding. And for those wanting to understand out of love and support for the survivors of domestic violence, this is for you, too.

Thank you for listening.

INTRODUCTION

I believe that in most—if not every—bad relationship, there comes a time when your brain and heart become torn. It's as if each of them is stitched to the other together like one big shirt. As the relationship wears, the seam that holds your brain and heart together wears as well. With just a little time, the shirt can tear right apart.

Your heart and brain in the beginning are playing for the same side; they fight together for love. They protect love; they each believe in it and let it blossom. But then, a small hole develops, becoming a tear between the two sides. This is when either the heart or brain decides it no longer feels the same as it once did, no longer wanting to play for the same team as its counterpart. It's exceedingly difficult because instead of your heart and brain consistently having two different viewpoints, they fight over what's right or wrong, good or bad—switching sides frequently. And the gnawing feeling that your brain disagrees with your heart follows you everywhere you go.

One day, your brain wakes up. I don't know if it's caused by a specific event, but you're suddenly awakened. Your eyes are no longer hidden by the veil. You now know that the relationship you are in is no longer safe, yet you are drowning in the turbulent waves that break against your body and soul. This phenomenon makes you question everything: your feelings, your future, your life, your current situation and how long it can or will last. On one side of the torn-up T-shirt is your heart, still clinging to the hope of love, hope for the future, not wanting to let go. Your heart tells you things will get better and that all will be well again. You still love each other and that is all you need. Perhaps if you love harder, try harder, give more and become better, he'll change and you will be happy together again.

The times I was alone, I struggled. There was a war raging inside of me and each side was just as powerful as the other. I was in constant turmoil. My brain hurt, my heart hurt—and they wouldn't stop. With each argument, my brain would think to leave, but my heart would protest in the name of love. My brain told me I was in a dangerous, unpredictable relationship and that I needed out. My heart would then tell me that I was exaggerating. It would say: *There are women out there in violent relationships much worse than mine.* When you tell yourself something enough, you start to believe it. And for a while, my heart won because I didn't want to throw in the towel.

By the time the relationship had become physically abusive, about one year in, I had put my entire being—blood, sweat and many tears—into the relationship and I didn't want to be a failure. So, I stayed. I know to many people this reasoning may sound silly and it is, especially looking back now, but in the moment, you can make the stupidest reasoning seem logical. For each person, it's a different reason—a child, not wanting to be alone or perhaps even financial security—but whatever the reason is to stay, no matter how stupid it may seem, it outweighs all the reasons to leave.

Furthermore, when you're in an abusive relationship, your actions have consequences. If you leave at the wrong time, you could suffer for it tremendously. That being said, there is almost never a right time or an opportunity to disappear. Max had convinced me that if I left him, he would kill himself. I believed him. I had seen him cut himself with my own eyes. I knew he was capable of causing harm to himself. I didn't want to be the reason for anyone to take their life. I would never have been able to forgive myself.

People don't see what they don't want to see. I didn't want to see Max as a monster. He was completely comfortable hitting, kicking, punching, choking and throwing knives at me, whether we were at home in private or out in the open. My brain would ask me every day if I still thought I loved this man and every day, I hesitated a little more to answer that question.

I had convinced myself that Max was just testing his boundaries, figuring out what he could get away with. *He didn't really want to hurt me. He was not going to kill me.* That's the kind of power someone can have over you. They make you think differently. My heart would remind me of all the times he had told me he loved me. *Sure, maybe sometimes he doesn't show it very well, but men are just like that. They are different from women when it comes to feelings and how they show love.* I had convinced myself for a long time that I exaggerated my stories, so I would play down the incidents.

I started believing that it was my fault, that I had said

or done something wrong that upset him and I should have known that he would react that way. *It was my fault, not his.* I didn't grasp the entirety of my situation and how bad it was.

Often after his abusive outbursts, Max would be so apologetic, almost humbled. He would tell me how much he loved me, needed me. He would tell me he'd die without me and that I made his life worth living. He told me he was so lucky to have me as only I knew the real Max yet still loved him unconditionally. He said he knew he was a monster, and therefore, I was his reason for living.

I loved the sweet, romantic, and nice Max who I truly believed was hiding just below the surface, but I rarely saw him. It was the monster Max that I hated and wanted to rid myself of. But how can you love someone and hate them at the same time? Which side do you listen to? Whose side do you choose?

This is my story.

CHAPTER 1

Sweet, Innocent, Naive

As a kid, I loved animals. I wanted to become a vet. At age fifteen, I had fallen behind in school as I hadn't liked the high school I was in. I was having a hard time trying to catch up, so I switched schools. Many students had, like me, struggled in the public school system and easily fallen behind. At this new school, I was finally finding my groove and doing well.

It was an alternative learning program set up in a business complex. The teachers cared for their students at this school. At all times, there were two or three teachers available who taught several subjects and whenever a student needed help, they were there for them. Students attended the school during three-hour time slots they were allowed to choose. They were expected to learn at their own pace, which eased a lot of the pressure. I was able to pick subjects I wanted to work on and when I wanted to work on them. At the end of my tenth-grade year, I won a Junior Academic Achievement Award, which was awesome because I had never won anything before. My parents were so proud of me. I was a vibrant girl without a care in the world.

The school consisted of three large connected rooms with desks and computers, a receptionist at the front and bathrooms and a kitchen in the back. We were allowed to use the school's kitchen to make lunch if we needed and they had an endless stockpile of tea we could help ourselves to while we studied. At this school, we didn't get lunch breaks since we were there for only a short time, but we were allowed two breaks of thirty minutes each where we could sit outside or go to the coffee shop next door.

There was a spot outside in one corner of the school where some kids would hang out and smoke. One day, I was frustrated with my math and had stepped outside for a short break. I sat down on a bench and looked out at the group of smokers. One particular boy was looking at me—a punk rocker–type with nose, lip and eyebrow piercings dressed in all black with ripped jeans at the calves and a large grungy hoodie.

He had the hood up, trying to look cool, I suppose. Under the hood was a horrible haircut: half his head was shaved and the other half was long. I had maybe only ever seen the boy once before. I wasn't sure if he was new or would come in for a later time slot than I did since my time slot for school was in the mornings. As time went on, I saw him more and more. I noticed him gradually start to come to school earlier each day. We never spoke, but we did make eye contact a few times.

One day, I was standing by the printer of one of the study rooms in frustration as the printer was not doing what I wanted it to do, and the boy came up to me. Little did I know at the time, this boy would become my boyfriend and a year later, my abuser.

"Hi," he said hurriedly and flustered, seeming not to know what to say. I was frustrated with the printer and not really looking for conversation. "Hi," I replied, not even lifting my head to look at him. He then proceeded to pretend like he knew what he was doing with the printer, but he was a fish out of water. He checked to make sure there was paper, which I had already done. Then, he opened the part covering the ink cartridges, as I had also already done. I ended up asking a teacher for help. When I went to sit back down after fighting long enough with the printer, my classmate came over to my desk. In a whispered rush, she demanded, "What did he say? Do you think he's cute?"

Not really knowing why she cared, I reluctantly replied, "He said hello." Reading her expression, I could tell it wasn't enough to quell her curiosity, so I added, "And I don't like his hair." We giggled and she went back to her seat. I went back to my English studies. That boy and I were obviously from two completely different worlds and our first encounter was nothing special.

He was a smoker, a rebel—the extreme opposite of me. I did not grow up in a house with drugs or alcohol, so that stuff never crossed my mind. I hung out with similar people, so I didn't have anyone trying to pressure me. I had good people around me. The occasional typical high school relationship would occur, but it never lasted very long and consisted of nothing more than holding hands and little kisses on the cheek. I was what you would call a good girl. And of course, like most good girls, I was a virgin. In no hurry, I was waiting for someone special to share that moment with.

CHAPTER 1

A couple of days later, he came and sat down next to me as I was doing my schoolwork. "Hi, I'm Max," he said, this time calm and collected. I figured he thought he'd give it another go. "Do you mind if I sit here?" he said as he pulled out a chair next to mine. Wondering what he was playing at, I stopped him with a "No, you can sit *there*," pointing at the chair across from me. I stood up, headed towards the kitchen for a cup of tea and muttered, "My name is Joy."

I came back to find Max had made himself comfortable in the chair next to mine—despite my resistance—and had his books decisively spread out. "What are you working on?" I asked flatly, almost forced, not quite convinced of his intentions. "English," he said, brushing his hair from his face. His hair was so long and his flinging it all over the place was quite distracting—not in a good way, but more in like a "get me a pair of scissors" kind of way.

"I don't know how you girls manage all your long hair," he joked. I didn't laugh. I was not impressed with him one bit. "They are called hair elastics," I said. He looked at me in a strange, unsure way.

I made a second suggestion in response: "If you don't like it, why don't you cut it off?" I wasn't nasty—just stating the obvious. "Do you not like my hair?" he asked broodingly. I looked up from my studies at his face to see if he was joking, but he was serious. I just looked down and shook my head no. "Oh," he let out sadly. The rest of the day, we sat in silence with our heads in our own books. He went outside for a smoke break every five minutes it seemed. He didn't end up staying long. One time, he went outside and didn't return.

The next day at school, I was in my regular seat doing my work when suddenly, this young man walked in. He looked familiar, but I couldn't place him. He seemed odd. He had a buzz cut and was wearing black pants and a black T-shirt. Out of nowhere, my friend who had swooned over him the day before came running over to me and sat on my desk. The weird smirk on her face caused me to inquire what was wrong with her. "What do you think?" she gushed as she gazed at the mysterious boy who had just walked into the classroom. She was dying to know. I must have looked puzzled. "That's Max!" she nearly shrieked.

I couldn't believe it. He looked entirely different. No more weird hair, no more hole-filled clothes. He even took out his eyebrow ring. I was shocked. My bewilderment must have been apparent. *Why would he do that?* I thought to myself.

"You know why, don't you?" she beamed so much it was unsettling. "He did it for you!" It burst out of her as if she couldn't contain herself. I looked back at the young man and realized it *was* him. I was astounded. He glanced at me quickly before walking into another study room.

He didn't come sit with me. He must have wanted me to watch him from afar. He was obvious in being aware of the fact that I was watching him and checking out his new look. He finally sat down and I got to really look at him.

In proper clothes and not so many holes in his face, he didn't look so bad. I even kind of thought that the lip ring he had left in was kind of sexy. He got up and went to the kitchen to make toast and I thought I'd ask him about it, so I got up and headed for the kitchen to make tea. "So, you cut your hair?" I said, not looking at him as I dipped my tea bag into a mug of steaming water.

"What do you think? Do you like it?" he asked with a slight smile, seeming pleased to show off his hair. "Well, it's definitely an improvement," I answered genuinely. He was looking for attention and I innocently gave it to him. I would soon learn that nothing good comes from stroking a young man's ego.

CHAPTER 2

This Could Be Love

As the days and eventual weeks followed, Max and I grew to become friends. We spoke often at school and when I needed a break, he would join me. We'd always sit together. We even took the same bus to and from school. I would go for walks in the park right across the road from the school. He started joining me on my little adventures and I enjoyed the company.

It was on one of these walks that he told me he had feelings for me. I don't remember my response, but it must have pleased him because we walked back to school hand in hand. I had butterflies in my stomach. He would take me to the coffee shop nearby and buy me tea or a hot chocolate. We would sit in the sun and talk until we'd forget the time and have to run back to school.

Once Max and I started hanging out together, the whole school, including the teachers, knew that we were a couple. Being the school couple was entirely new to me. It was interesting. I was in the spotlight a lot of the time. Eventually, our teachers prevented us from sitting together because they claimed we weren't getting enough done, which was probably true. But it was all in fun. We would pass notes to each other with the help of our friends.

Sometimes, Max would walk by my desk and kneel behind the desk out of the teacher's sight. We would talk quietly until a teacher would turn their head in our direction and frown at us. He would then slowly slink away back to where he was supposed to be seated.

I had told Max that I wanted to go slow. It was scary the feelings that would arise in me when he was around. Before Max, I had only ever French-kissed a boy once and it was terrible. I had never experienced wanting to be close to someone all the time and the emptiness that would possess me if he didn't sneak a glance in my direction several times throughout the school day. I felt like I was really starting to fall in love with him, hard and fast.

CHAPTER 2

He made me feel special. He would pick flowers for me on our walks and put them in my hair, all the while complimenting me. The feelings were strong and consuming. A thought that scared me was the fact that he had more experience than I did. I had confided in Max that I was a virgin and he had been very respectful and seemed to know and understand that I was waiting for a special moment with a special person. I thought that he had acted quite gentlemanly about it. He had cut his hair for me and I asked him if he wouldn't smoke cigarettes around me as it bothered me, and he had pretty much quit. In my head, he was doing all this stuff for me because he truly cared about me. He really seemed like the real deal. He was so kind and patient. He never pushed me to do anything, and I didn't feel rushed, although deep down I knew that things would progress.

Our first kiss was shared on one of our breaks. We had gone for a walk. It was a beautiful, sunny, warm day. I was sitting on a rock, basking in the sun, just enjoying being out of the classroom for a little bit. Max was pacing back and forth nervously.

"What's wrong?" I asked, concerned. "Come sit next to me. Relax. Enjoy the warm sun," I suggested. He came and sat next to me, wrapping his arms around me, pulling me close. We were both looking deep into each other's eyes, and I could feel my heart beating in my throat. I had wanted to kiss him but I was so nervous that as he leaned in to kiss me, I shyly turned my head so that he kissed my cheek and not my lips.

After my first unpleasant kissing encounter, I was afraid I'd be a bad kisser. He tenderly put his hands on my cheeks and kissed me softly on the lips. It was so gentle and loving. He leaned back and looked at me. He had beautiful steel blue eyes. I could feel a warm sensation creeping up my face as I became flushed and smiled at him. He kissed me again, this time more passionately. Every kiss was better than the last and I was able to relax. It was as if he was guiding me and I simply followed. When he gently brushed his tongue past my lips and I felt it on my tongue, I was a little surprised, but I slightly parted my lips and let him in. And just as quickly as it had happened, it was over. He gave me a quick kiss on the cheek before standing up and holding his hand out to me. I reached for him and stood up. We walked back to school holding hands in silence. I couldn't stop smiling. I had finally had a real meaningful and loving kiss.

Soon after our kiss in the park, our relationship seemed to be more official than just a school crush. He became more serious about being my boyfriend and we began spending more time together outside of school. He would hang out sometimes with me and a couple of my girlfriends as we went downtown to go shopping or simply find a spot to hang out together. He introduced me to all the smokers at school and sometimes I would go out with him during his smoke breaks and chat with him and his friends. Once he had introduced me to his mother and little sister, I went to his house often. His mother was a very busy single mum. She was always working and his little sister would always be at friends' houses, so we spent a lot of time alone at his house. We would spend hours in his room lying on the bed facing each other talking or listening to music. His favourite band was Hedley, and he would sing to me.

My mother was always eager to meet the boys that either my sister or I dated, so I introduced her to Max. She didn't think much of him as I could tell, and seemed to think it wouldn't last long, but, nonetheless, she let us do our thing as long as I obeyed the house rules. There were, however, a lot of rules.

My mother would not let us hang out unsupervised and if we were in my bedroom, I always had to have the bedroom door open. Needless to say, he didn't like to spend much time at my house. He was used to no rules and being allowed to do pretty much whatever he wanted at his house.

Whenever we were at his place alone, we would play house. We would grocery shop and cook together. It was fun and something I had never done before. It felt very natural as the music played and we cooked and chatted in the kitchen. I had told Max that I was the kind of girl who loved romantic gestures—the flowers, going out for dinners and all the cheesy things that couples do. I had watched one too many chick flicks for sure, and I wanted the fairytale romance from the movies.

One day, Max went out with a friend on a small fishing boat. The boys were gone all day setting crab traps and checking them. He came back to his house with two huge crabs and boiled them for dinner. It was a total surprise.

He had simply told me he had a special night planned and that I would love it and to be at his house by 5 p.m. When I showed up at his house, the table was perfectly set with a fancy tablecloth, candles and a beautiful bouquet of colourful flowers in the center. There was quiet classical music playing in the background and the lights in the house were dimmed. The setting was that of an upscale restaurant. I was completely awestruck. He had put in so much effort to make this a special evening. He took my coat off at the door and led me inside.

There was a bottle of red wine he had gotten from his mother and there were beautiful crystal glasses on the table. I was swept off my feet. It was such a romantic gesture, and no one had ever done anything like that for me before.

The evening was perfect. The food was delicious, and I felt very special. Afterwards, we cuddled on the couch and watched a movie. The evening, however, would have to come to an end. I could never stay too late as I had a curfew, and I was not allowed to sleep over at his house; those were my mother's rules.

Soon, he was introducing me to his friends as his girlfriend, which at that age always makes you feel special. They were like him; they drank and smoked, but they included me in their group. One day, Max, a friend of his and I went for a walk down to the beach. We sat on a rock in the sun. His friend pulled out a six-pack of Budweiser. We were all underage, but Max had mentioned there was a guy who always hung around the liquor stores who would get you the beer and keep the change.

I had never drunk beer or any liquor before. Max handed me a can and I took it. I didn't want to seem rude or uncool and I felt, as most young kids do, the desire to fit in. The boys started drinking their beer, so I opened mine and gingerly took a small sip. Max looked at me as he knew I didn't drink. I smiled, trying to make it look like I was enjoying it. After some time when the boys were caught up in their conversation, I dumped the beer and pretended I had drunk it.

One day, we were at Max's house alone as usual and we had just finished watching a romantic movie (I love my romantic movies). We were kissing, and it became more and more passionate. He picked me up off the couch and carried me upstairs and into the bedroom. He put me down and locked the door behind us. I knew this was going to be the moment. I loved Max and he loved me, and I really wanted him to make love to me.

He took off his shirt and I looked at his somewhat chiseled chest. I had seen it before, of course, but now everything felt new. He wrapped me in his arms and told me he wouldn't do anything that I didn't want. At the time, to me, this meant respect. He gently laid me back on the bed as he was kissing down my neck and the tops of my breasts. I felt very nervous as he reached around to undo my bra and slowly removed it. He pulled the covers up and over the both of us, smiling at me sweetly. "Are you sure you want to do this?" he asked me tenderly while holding a condom. I nodded yes shyly and kissed him. That was my first time.

It wasn't steamy and hot like in movies, but I don't think anyone's first time is. Afterwards, we lay there covered in sweat, him holding me in his arms. "I love you," he whispered. All I could think about was how tired I was and the fact that I was no longer a virgin. It was kind of a crazy thing to think about. We napped for an hour or so and then we took a shower together. We were typical teenagers, discovering sex and what it was all about.

Actually, we were more like rabbits. Every day, sometimes several times a day, we couldn't get enough of each other. We had been together for almost a year by that point, and I was completely enamoured with the idea of being high school sweethearts who would get married and grow old together. And that is what I had hoped for Max and me.

At the same time, my infatuation was getting me in trouble with my mum. I had always followed the house rules, but I had begun to miss my curfew often. Once, I called my mum and told her that I had fallen asleep during a movie and that I had missed the last bus. It was a lie, but there really were only two buses that went by Max's house, and they ran at very inconvenient hours. So, that night, I spent the night at Max's. His mother could have cared less.

Then, the lies became more and more frequent. I had never lied to my mother before. I really loved her, but at this point, I was growing up and I felt like she was still trying to treat me like a young girl. So, I lied to her.

"The bus never showed up."

"The bus was early."

"I missed the bus. I fell asleep again!"

Any excuse I could think of. After a while, my mother stopped expecting me to come home, so I just didn't go home at all. It was summer and school was out, so we were always out hanging with his friends or just hanging out at the house.

One day, we went over to his friend's house, someone I had met a couple of times. He was a great guy and we clicked right away, but he was a complete stoner. The first time I ever got high, I had simply walked into his house. The smoke hung in the air, on the closed curtains. It was almost hard to see through. Like a Turkish bath house but no old naked men and instead of thick steam, it was thick smoke.

We sat on the couch and the boys took turns smoking from a big bong, another thing I had never done. After maybe ten minutes, I was already high. I could feel it. I felt kind of giddy and silly—overly happy and I didn't know

CHAPTER 2

why. My mouth was as dry as the Sahara Desert. My head was spinning, and it all seemed somewhat surreal to me. I asked the boys if we could go get food as I was hungry. They both laughed. I didn't understand at the time. We left and went to McDonald's.

Max was a whole different person when other people were around. It was odd, but I figured boys didn't want to look like total puppy dogs in front of their friends. When we were with his friends, he was often indifferent towards me, but when it was just the two of us, it was like I was his whole world. It was like he couldn't get enough of me.

CHAPTER 3

A Different Side Emerges

That summer, Max got me a job working with him at a Greek restaurant. He told me that he had worked the previous year's busy season and that the boss and his wife had seemed to really like him. He was the dishwasher and helped with food prep. I started by doing most of the dishes while he did most of the prep. I enjoyed it for the most part. It was easy and the days went by quickly as it was a busy restaurant. After work, a lot of the staff would sit around the bar and drink. Max would often help himself to a beer, which the boss seemed to ignore, but I wasn't comfortable with that. After all, we were underaged.

As the days went by, I learned more and more about prepping the food as well as taking care of the dishes. I would polish the silverware and glasses for the servers when they got busy. One day, there was a big party scheduled and they needed more help. The boss asked me if I would bus tables after Max and I had finished all the prepping. I was very excited. It was a new responsibility and I was up to the challenge.

The evening went smoothly. I began by setting all the tables for the party. During the party, it was my job to keep the wine glasses full and clear the dishes as soon as customers were finished. When the party started to die down and I had removed the last dish from the table, there were only a few remaining guests savouring their drinks and chatting.

I headed back to the dish pit to finish up the last of the dishes. It was quite late, and Max had left long before to catch a bus home. It was probably three hours or so before the dishes were all done and put away and the party area had been cleaned and put back to normal, ready for the next day. Only a few people stayed and hung around the bar that night.

My boss' wife, Vicki, pulled me aside as I was heading towards the bar at the front of the restaurant. She praised me for my hard work and asked me if I wanted to work the front of the house more often, especially on other busy nights. I told her I would love to. She also offered me more shifts, which meant more money, so I agreed. I told Max the next day that Vicki had offered me more shifts and he said he was happy for me. He knew I loved helping and being needed. From then on, I worked five nights a week and Max worked two of those nights. At first, it was kind of weird being there without him as he was the reason I had the job, but I quickly got used to it and really enjoyed the diversity in tasks I performed at the restaurant. Life went on as normal.

Max was always on-again, off-again with the smoking. He knew I hated it, especially since every time we had sex, afterwards he would go down for a smoke. But by this time, we had found liquor that I liked. I discovered vodka and tequila. He had his poison and now I had mine. I had also started to smoke weed. I even bought myself my very own pipe. It had beautiful colours. I was quite proud of my little pipe. Whenever I did go home—basically just to get new clothes—my mother would complain that I smelt of weed. She claimed to be allergic to it. I would tell her that I had been downtown and that there were a bunch of people smoking weed. Other times, I would just outright deny it. She would glare at me as she sniffed up and down my body like a drug dog. It irritated me so much, this whole routine of hers.

By this time, I had isolated myself, nondeliberately and unknowingly, from my girlfriends. I was always with Max's friends or working. Since it was summer, I didn't have school as a reason to see my friends every day. My girlfriends called me one day and told me that they were upset that they never saw me anymore. I also missed my girl time. So, we made a pact that every Tuesday would be girls' day—no boys allowed. I would hang out with Max all week, but Tuesdays were reserved for girls' day.

We would shop, go for walks in the park, and sometimes, we would go to one of our houses—not mine—and watch chick flicks while eating ice cream. My two best friends were just like how I was before I met Max. They did not party, drink, or smoke and they were still virgins. I told them of some of the new experiences that I had had but not too many details because I felt like I was a completely different person compared to who I was the year before. I felt like I couldn't relate to them so much anymore, but they were still my girls. I still enjoyed my time with them. We had all attended school together, so they had met Max but didn't really know him as most of my time with him was spent just the two of us.

CHAPTER 3

Every week on Tuesday, us girls got together and did whatever we wanted. I had explained to Max that sometimes I just missed being with my old friends and it was nice to have girl time. He respected that he was not allowed to come, although he didn't like it.

It was the beginning of a new week and I was really looking forward to girls' day when Max began begging and pleading to tag along. I told him he would have no fun unless he wanted to carry all of our shopping bags. I told him that I had made a pact with the girls that boys weren't allowed. But, he was determined. I did not know why at the time. I figured maybe with me working more he was feeling a little lonely or neglected.

The following day was Tuesday. I called the girls and told them that Max really wanted to join us on our girls' day. I promised them it would only happen this one time. They were not happy about it, but because they wanted to hang out with me, they complied.

We hung out in a park just talking and Max would just sit there sucking on his stupid cigarette. To a regular passerby, I'm sure he seemed out of place with these girls chatting away on the other side of the bench. Nevertheless, it was a good night and we enjoyed ourselves. When Max wanted to go home, we ended the evening. I told the girls

I'd see them next Tuesday—"without Max," I whispered—and hugged them as they got on their bus to go home.

The following week, Max told me he had something special planned for me. He had reservations at a beautiful little Italian restaurant downtown. This place was booked up, but they had had a cancellation Tuesday night and could fit us in. I reminded him that Tuesday night was girls' night, so he'd have to change the reservations.

"Babe, I made these reservations two weeks ago. I can't change them. We were lucky to get in. You can have girls' night next week. It's not a big deal," he said defensively. Just then, changing his tone to a loving one, he said, "You love getting all dressed up and doing romantic things." I did love all those things, so I hoped the girls would understand. But I knew that if I told them I was bailing on them to be with Max, they would be upset with me. So, I lied about why Tuesday wouldn't work for girls' day. The girls were pretty upset. I think they saw right through my lies. I felt like shit as I was not a liar, but by that point, I was lying to pretty much everybody who cared about me.

Tuesday night, we both got dressed up. I wore a long, dazzling gown and Max wore slacks and a dress shirt. I had never seen him look so elegant. Man, was he handsome when he tried. When we arrived at the restaurant, there was a huge line outside on the street. A friend had recommended this restaurant and obviously everyone else loved it, too.

We were two complete lovebirds waiting in line, sharing passionate kisses and whispering sweet nothings in each other's ears. He made me blush with the sweet compliments he was giving me. I felt so grown up and I liked that. We had never done anything like this before, so I was quite swept away by the evening.

The restaurant was small and a little crowded, but the atmosphere was idyllic: candles everywhere, cozy seating and the finest fare. First, we had fresh baked bread with olive oil and vinegar to dip. Then, we had amazing pasta for dinner and for dessert, we shared a piece of cheesecake. After dinner, Max took me for a walk along the harbour. It was breathtaking. The gardens and the walkway along the water were illuminated with gleaming white lights. In the air was the sound of boats gently rocking in the water as a warm breeze blew through the boat riggings. The night was magical. I was blissful, and I thought life couldn't get any better than this. I felt genuinely loved and special.

After our walk along the water, we walked to the bus stop. I sat on his warm lap and we held hands as I rested my head on his shoulders, feeling so in love. We kept smiling at each other and all I could think about was how much I really loved Max and how much he must have loved me to do all this for me.

When we arrived at his house, it was dark and silent. Everyone was already in bed. We went upstairs and made passionate love, which was the perfect way to end the perfect evening. And it had been the perfect evening, that is, until he kissed me and told me he'd be right back.

He had gone downstairs. I heard the front door of the house close quietly. I looked out the window and there was Max sitting outside smoking, talking to a friend on the phone. He had pretended to quit when we first got together. He used to hide it from me, but now he didn't really hide it anymore. I told him I wanted him to stop, but what could I do? I was absolutely smitten by this boy, and I figured no one was perfect. Maybe it would just take a little longer. I made myself believe that if I loved him enough and he loved me back, he would quit.

Smoking wasn't his only vice. He was a partier. He liked to go out with his buddies late at night and wander the streets drunk and be loud and rowdy. Most of those nights I was either working, alone at his house or I would be at my house. I grew up in a house with parents who didn't drink at all, so his lifestyle was quite different from what I was used to.

Max also liked to use drugs recreationally. His drug of choice was cocaine. He never did it in front of me. He would do it when I was at work or school. He'd go out with his buddies and call me at three o'clock in the morning and I could tell he was not himself. I was always worried about the trouble he could get himself into.

It seemed almost every day we'd be sitting at his friend's house on the couch smoking pot. We both began to smoke a lot. My mother was starting to get more and more on my nerves when I went home, which was rare. I always felt like I was being interrogated. My mother would ask me all sorts of questions about the people I was with and the things we would do.

She would accuse me of doing drugs and drinking, which wasn't entirely untrue, but she made it sound much worse than it was. She no longer trusted me, and she said she didn't know who I was anymore. Once, she made me so angry, I yelled some horrible things to her. I was leaving the house and I told her that the reason she was so upset was because she wasn't having sex and I told her that maybe she should go get some. I don't know why I thought that would be a smart thing to say but teenagers say stupid meaningless things. Looking back, I regret every stupid, bitchy, degrading thing I ever said to her. After I had said my piece, I slammed the door shut behind me and headed towards the bus stop to go back to Max's house.

By this time, I had been working at the Greek restaurant for maybe two months. One night, Max and I went into work together. It was his first shift in two weeks. The restaurant had begun to cut some of his shifts, so he hardly worked at that point.

When I arrived at work, Vicki, the boss' wife, pulled me aside and said, "Max isn't working out for us any longer and we are seriously considering letting him go. Would you consider picking up his shifts?"

I was dumbfounded. I didn't know what to say. I thought they had been cutting his shifts because the summer was soon ending and the restaurant was less busy, but it appeared that I was mistaken and they were trying to weed him out. I wasn't sure if I should take my boyfriend's job. That didn't seem like something a good girlfriend would or should do. "I don't know, Vicki. I don't think Max would like it if I took his job," I replied.

"Its your choice, but we are letting him go and we would like you to stay and take extra work if possible. Let me know. I'll give you time to think about it," she said curtly as she opened the door for me to enter the kitchen. As I entered the dish pit, Max seemed to already be in a bad mood

CHAPTER 3

as he aggressively organized his station, throwing pots and pans around and soaking the floors with the sprayer. I had to put salt on the ground to keep myself from slipping all over the place. I decided to avoid him for a while because I didn't want him to ask me what Vicki had wanted to talk about.

CHAPTER 4

Losing Control

*I*t had been maybe thirty minutes since we had arrived at work. Max went to the bar to get some water and then went outside for a smoke break. I saw Vicki go outside after him. I could hear what sounded like arguing going on, but I couldn't make out any words that were exchanged. Suddenly, the back door was thrown open and Max came in like a tornado headed in my direction. He grabbed my arm and started pulling me towards the door. "Come on. We're leaving," he commanded. "What do you mean we're leaving? What happened? We have work to do," I soberly responded.

"No, we don't. We're quitting. They don't want either of us here anymore," he replied assuredly as the back door slammed shut behind us.

"Max, listen. I like this job. I don't want to leave. I know they are cutting hours since it isn't the busy season anymore, but Vicki has asked me to stay, and I would really like to. Maybe I can become a server and make tips," I said, trying to show him how the job offer would honestly only help us both in the end, but it wasn't a strong enough reason for his ego to overlook the slight.

"Did they offer you my job—my shifts?" he demanded, glaring at me. I didn't know what to say. I had never seen him angry like this before and it was slightly scary. I really didn't want to tell him Vicki had offered me his job, but I also wasn't a liar. He would know if I lied to him.

"I'll go in and talk to Vicki, okay? We'll work this out. It'll be okay. You aren't going to lose your job." I ran back inside quickly and saw Vicki standing in the kitchen talking to the chef.

"I'm so sorry about this, Vicki. Max will be leaving but I'll stay and work the dinner rush," I said to her apologetically. Max came back in through the door and marched right up to Vicki.

"Vicki, we quit. As in her and I." He looked at me sharply. "We are leaving. Now." Once again, he grabbed me and pulled me away. I felt helpless. I really didn't know what to do. I didn't want to upset Max. I felt that I should go with my boyfriend. I let him pull me towards the back door and as he opened it and pulled me outside, I looked back at Vicki one last time.

"You are going to regret this. If you leave now, you can never come back looking for a job. I wouldn't leave if I were you. You're going to fucking regret this," she shouted at me angrily. I was shocked and just as quickly as it had started, the door was shut and it was over. I stood outside the door for a little while in complete shock.

I no longer had a job and Vicki had shouted and swore at me. Max pulled at my hand, and we began to walk to the bus stop towards home. The bus ride home was quiet. I kept going over the events in my head, wondering, *Did that just really happen?*

Max was beginning to isolate me. I never really spoke with my mother or any family. I only saw my friends at school at that point and when I did see them, they wouldn't greet me the way they used to. I felt like a stranger amongst my own friends, which led me back to Max because that was where I felt safe and loved. My friends clearly didn't want anything to do with me anymore. On the other hand, his friends, though they were not my typical crowd, accepted me and I needed that. Girls' days were long gone, so now it was Max twenty-four hours a day, seven days a week. I was so in love, or so I thought, that I never noticed that it was me letting him push my friends away and, in my mind, my friends were cold to me and I didn't know why. I didn't understand why they didn't want to hang out with me.

Max would say they were jealous because we loved each other. Max would follow me around school and always made sure to sit next to me. I was like a puppet with strings. He would tell me what we were doing that day and that's what we would do. He had my schedule all planned out around him and what was convenient for him.

I wish now looking back that I had paused and thought to myself, *Wait a second. I am my own person, and I should be making my own choices.* But instead, I was a helpless puppet and I never said anything. I wanted to be the girlfriend who didn't manage or boss around her boyfriend. And because the decisions seemed small—where to sit in school or what to do after school—I went with the flow. Never making decisions myself, I always went along with what Max wanted to do.

Back at school, I was doing my work experience course. I had always wanted to become a vet, so I got to do my work experience at an animal clinic not far from school. I loved it. I was happy to have something other than school and my annoying mother in my life as well as my full-time job of a relationship. It was a rare moment that Max wasn't next to me. I thought it was kind of sweet that he was checking up on me, but it was a constant thing. He never made it sound like he was keeping tabs on me. He would sometimes use his friends to keep track of me, but it's not like I had anything to hide. He would often use his friends' cell phones to call me, even when I was doing my work experience at the vet clinic, or he would get them to call me to see where I was.

I felt a bit smothered, so work had become my escape. At work, I could be myself. I worked with some nice people, and they seemed to like me. It was a very healthy environment for me to be in. I loved the work. I was hoping that after my work experience, they would hire me. I worked hard and went above and beyond. I knew they were hiring, and I voiced my interest in the position to my supervisor.

After my sixty hours of work experience, they hired me on as a Boarding Attendant, so my job duties included basic care of the animals who were boarding as well as those recovering from surgery. I walked the dogs twice a day in a beautiful park right next to the clinic. I was at school during the day, and I worked on weekends. I already had my eye on the next position up from me: the Veterinary Assistant.

I wanted to work in the Trauma section of the hospital. I tried to help in the Trauma area as much as possible whenever I had caught up on my daily tasks.

At my house, the relationship between my mother and I was becoming more and more strained and hostile. One night, my mum and I got into a huge fight. She wasn't going to let me leave the house. She grabbed me and wouldn't let go. I was struggling and fighting with her. I yelled at her, pushed her and told her I hated her. I will never forget that day. It haunts me the way I treated her. I kept threatening to move out. I was tired of being treated like a child and having to follow her rules. I felt as though I was old enough to know how to care for myself as I had money saved from working so much and I thought that I was balancing life quite well.

Max and I started talking about moving in together. He thought it was a great idea and strongly encouraged me to find a place we could move into. We had a plan in which he would get a job and I could work more hours. We'd live cheaply to save money and have our very own place together with no one to bug us or tell us what to do. I had some money saved up and I no longer wanted to be going back and forth between Max's house and mine. We decided that my mother was too much of a hassle and caused me a lot of stress, so for my health and sanity, we started looking for apartments.

We looked in the newspapers and online. It was quite difficult, two sixteen-year-olds looking for an apartment with no previous experience living on their own. We looked at a few places, but they all fell through. After weeks of rejection after rejection, it became very disheartening. I was mortified at the thought of having to live with my mother forever. Most places wanted references from previous landlords, which we did not have, as well as proof of employment, which Max didn't have. I was desperate, so one day I called my father with whom I hadn't spoken in a while. We were not the closest and we rarely saw eye to eye. He happened to have a house that had an upstairs suite which could house three tenants with a shared bathroom, kitchen and living area.

My father had one tenant and two empty bedrooms. I figured it would be a good start, even just temporarily, until we found something better suited for us. The tenant was a bachelor who was often gone and the place needed a bit of work, but I asked my father if he would rent it out to Max and I. My father, like my mother, was not a fan of Max but he had not seen my transformation in the year I had been with Max, so he wasn't aware of all the red flags.

CHAPTER 5

Struggling to Be Independent

It took a couple of days for my father to let us know, but we eventually agreed on $600 a month and rent had to be paid—no exceptions. It didn't take me long to pack my clothes and other important articles as well as my pet cat and we moved in. We went to the dollar store and bought kitchen utensils, plates and all sorts of household items. Furniture we found in thrift shops and on the internet. Soon, we had our cozy little home all set up.

I paid for everything. I supported both Max and I until he could find a job. I even bought him dress pants and a shirt to wear to job interviews. I didn't mind because I knew that soon enough, we'd both be making money and then we could save the rest after paying for food and rent and such. During the day, I would go to school and then to work afterwards. I would help Max out on the job front by looking at the classifieds online and Craigslist for job ads and I would print his resumes at school so we didn't have to pay for the paper like we would at a public library.

I finally felt happy. I had a place of my own, I was making my own money and I felt very grown up. One thing I never considered was the bills: hydro, internet, on top of phones and bus transport and with Max not having found a job, I was paying all his bills too. For food, we shopped at the dollar store and lived mostly off of Mr. Noodles instant ramen.

Once a week, we were able to go to the community food bank and get a bag of groceries, one per person. We managed, although the dollar store and the food bank never had fresh produce or meat. It was all canned goods and packaged products. You were lucky to get a day-old loaf of bread, but those were few and far between. If you got there early enough in the morning, sometimes there was bread left over from a bakery that donated the bread at the end of the day to the food bank. In the morning, the bread would be on the counter and each family could choose one thing of bread. I rarely got there early enough, so we didn't get

CHAPTER 5

bread often. It took a toll on my health after months of eating packaged and canned food. My skin began to grey.

Once I had saved some money, I went to the grocery store instead of the dollar store to see what I could get. I didn't have a lot, so I thought I could just grab some necessities and maybe if I had a little extra, I could get some chocolate or ice cream. I walked up and down all the aisles, noticing all the foods I used to be able to afford and could afford no longer. I reminisced about the good old times with all this fancy food.

I had never before in my life experienced a time when I could not afford simple pleasures. I was never a rich person growing up, but my mother let my sister and I enjoy sugary cereals occasionally and other more expensive items. Cheese was a luxury I could no longer afford, and it was greatly missed.

I decided not to be greedy and get only what I needed. I grabbed a gallon of milk, a loaf of bread and a box of cereal. I was walking through the meat aisle towards the cash registers when I noticed some cheap steaks. *How I would kill for a nice juicy steak*, I thought to myself. I decided that instead of ice cream I would grab a small steak for Max and I to share. I was so excited to go home and have a real piece of meat.

I arrived at the cash register with the shortest line and put my items on the conveyor belt. The line went quickly and soon the girl started ringing me up. I was watching her ring up my items when I realized I would have to leave the steak behind. *That's okay*, I thought to myself, *I don't need it. It's frivolous anyway.*

"I won't be taking the steak. Sorry. I forgot I already have something for dinner tonight." I said to her apologetically but trying to sound as if it wasn't a big deal. I handed her the tiny package with a sad little piece of steak in it. I didn't need or want anyone knowing the real reason I couldn't buy the steak was I had no money.

She finished ringing up my items and gave me the total. Even without the steak, I didn't have enough. I handed her the milk. "Sorry, I guess I'll leave this with you as well." She adjusted the bill without the milk and read me the new total. It was maybe a dollar more than I had. I took the cereal out of the bag that she had already packed it in and handed it to her. "You can take this off the bill. Sorry." By this time, I was quite embarrassed. *I shouldn't have gone to a grocery store. I should have stuck with dollar store food*, I thought. There were people standing in line behind me and I couldn't help but wonder what they must have thought of this pathetic girl who couldn't afford food. I just wanted to get out of there. I considered leaving everything and just running out. I decided to muster up my strength and hold the little dignity I had.

I handed her just the money for the bread, but she quickly packed all the items I had returned to her in the same bag as the bread. I looked up at this girl who was probably not much older than I. "Just go," she said kindly. I stared at her bewildered. She was asking me to take the unpaid items and leave. That was stealing. I have never stolen anything in my life. "Are you sure?" I asked. "Won't you get in trouble—fired even?"

"Don't worry about it. I can tell you're going through a rough patch," she said in the nicest way. I couldn't believe someone would be so nice to me, a total stranger. I looked at the people behind me in line thinking one of them might say something or try to stop me, but they didn't even seem to notice. The girl behind the till still smiling sweetly gave a little nod with her head towards the door as if to say, "*Now get outta here!*"

"Thank you so very much," I said to her quietly before leaving the store. As soon as I was out the door and around the corner, I slumped against the brick wall and began to cry. I was so grateful for this girl's kindness, but I also felt ashamed. Was this who I had become? A pathetic loser who now depended on other people's generosity to be able to feed herself? A lowlife, a beggar almost. I thought of other people who suffered even greater than I who would kill for this food. This food was now even more valuable than its price tag. After a few minutes of sulking, I collected myself and headed home with my groceries. I didn't go back to that grocery store for years as I was afraid that someone would remember me.

Heading home, I tried to cheer up and I thought about what I could combine with the steak to make a beautifully delicious dinner for Max and I. When I got home, Max wasn't there, so I decided to start on dinner. I cooked rice from a package and warmed canned vegetables, all from the dollar store. I then seasoned the steak with salt and pepper and cooked it medium rare, my favourite. I waited for Max to get home so we could eat together. I kept the food warm while I waited, but time was passing quickly and then it was dark. I served a plate for myself and then I covered a plate with aluminum foil for Max. I sat down at the table by myself, looking out the window so I could see Max when he got home. I left him more food than I gave myself.

He got home late that night and he was drunker than drunk. "How was your day?" I asked him, "Did you hand out a lot of resumes?" He looked at me with glazed eyes. "I was at a friend's house," he slurred, "Taking a break from all the job hunting. It doesn't allow much time for me to relax." I asked him where he had gotten the money to get that drunk. "Me and Eddie were just walking around and since it is recycling day, everyone has their recycling boxes out on the curb. So, we decided to collect the bottles for cash. We were collecting all day. He needs the cash. He said if I helped him, my split of the profit would be a pack of smokes and then some food," he said proudly.

"And you never thought to save any of it for us, for food, bills or your bus fare?" He shot me a look as if to deem me unappreciative that he had fed himself for once. After polishing off the sandwich he brought home, he casually wandered to the bedroom, flopped onto the bed and passed out. Another selfish act of his. He chose to get drunk for one night and buy cigarettes instead of buy food or help in any way when he knew I was supporting us and running extremely low on funds.

Somehow, I managed to pay all the bills and feed us at the same time, although it became extremely hard, and some days were downright miserable. Being an adult was much harder than I thought. I felt free from parents, and I was finally able to be my own person, but I felt the strain of having to support a deadbeat boyfriend. Max and I were arguing more and more. We both had started to become affected by the stress of being independent.

When we moved out on our own, Max slowly changed and his behaviour became more controlling. I thought that I knew his vices and had accepted them for the most part. I knew he would likely never quit smoking no matter how many times he tried. He had tried the nicotine patch, but he said it gave him nightmares and night sweats. He had tried smoking menthol cigarettes because they were so disgusting as to deter someone from smoking, but he ended up liking them, so that didn't work. He also tried quitting cold turkey but then he'd be with friends and when they would smoke, he would always partake.

I caught him multiple times sneaking outside for a smoke, so I figured I just had to learn to accept it. He also liked to drink. He spent less time at school, and he was constantly at his friend's house. I thought it was weird at first that he would spend his days at an older woman's house who lived in a cheap housing complex. Every day. The house was messy and stunk of cigarettes and weed. Whenever I was there with him, which was often, we would just sit around. I would chat with Max and his friend as they smoked cigarette after cigarette, and once in a while, we'd all share a joint. It wasn't fun like my girls' days had been. But that's what he did day in and day out, and I joined him occasionally as he liked having me around.

Max went to school less and less, claiming he was out job hunting. He would only show up to use the school computers to look for jobs and create resumes, so I had no reason to believe that he wasn't trying his best to find a job. One big problem, though, was he didn't have a cell phone, so there was no contact information for possible employers. He always seemed to lose his phone or it would break during his drunken escapades. We put my number on his resume so at least people could call me and I could give him the message and he could call them back.

When I wasn't with him, he always managed to find a phone to call and check up on me. He would say that he had dropped by a friend's house quickly and thought to call me. He would ask me where I was, what I was doing and when I'd be home—questions that would seem somewhat normal, but they were all too frequent. Young, naive me thought it was cute. I thought he missed me and wanted to make sure I was okay, or maybe he just wanted to hear my voice. So, despite some of my doubts, I pretended it was nothing.

Some nights I'd come home from work and Max would still be out. I wouldn't have any way to contact him as he could be literally anywhere, so I would usually wait around for him. I hated it when I'd make a nice dinner that I was quite proud of and I'd want to eat it together with him, but he wasn't home. He always did come home eventually, though. And when he did, I would ask him about his day and his answers were always, "I was out," "At a friend's," or just plain "fine." But I never heard anything about jobs, interviews or even places at which he might have dropped off resumes. No one had called to ask for him either.

I took on more hours at work as our money situation became tighter. We were going through my savings quicker than I thought we would as I was hoping Max would have a job by now. With the phone bill, the bus fares and all the other bills, we were barely scraping by. I asked him a few times if he could possibly pick up some of the house duties, like dinner, dishes and basic housekeeping since I was working more and had less time and he could do that until he found a job. He always said yes but then I'd come home and the kitchen would be a mess from him making a simple sandwich.

There'd be jars of peanut butter and jam open with a dirty knife on the counter. The bathroom would have towels on the floor from after he showered. I'd walk into the bedroom and he'd be sitting there playing video games. He'd look at me and ask about my day casually as if it didn't look like a tornado ran through the place. The floor would be littered with clothes and dirty dishes. I'd be so upset, but I didn't know what else to do. I would go to the bathroom and sit on the edge of the bathtub and cry. It was not the life I had signed up for. I was horribly disappointed that he didn't seem to care anymore. And then after maybe an hour of crying in the bathroom, I would wash my face, have a shower and go to bed like nothing was wrong.

Then, the next day, he would be super sweet and loving towards me. Max could be very convincing at times. We'd cuddle in bed and watch a movie together. We'd have amazing sex and I would feel so in love again. Then, we'd have a shower together, washing each other. I'd head to the kitchen to make food for us and he would sit by the front door with a cigarette in his mouth and we'd chat for a while. These moments made me feel incredibly special and loved. I began to think it hadn't been too long living this way and I thought I just needed to be patient and give him time. I would dream about living in a nice house and I even flirted with the idea of marriage. I always felt happy in those precious moments, though there weren't too many of them. I convinced myself that once Max found a full-time job and we started saving money, the relationship wouldn't be so hard.

One day, Max went to go visit his buddy who worked at a Subway not too far from our house. It was a day off for me, which I rarely got, so I slept in. When I woke up, Max was sitting by the kitchen window eating a Subway sandwich. He would get free sandwiches from his buddy at work when the boss wasn't around. He could go in there and order anything at all for free—and he did frequently. In the early days of our relationship, we had gone to that same Subway and his friend had made us a footlong sandwich to share: half had my toppings and half had his.

But on this day, there was no food in the fridge, so I asked him if I could have a bite, but as I said it, he wolfed down the last bit and gave me a look like, "Sorry, none left." I was so hurt that he would not share what little food there was. He told me that he was only allowed one free sandwich and he never thought to share, then he went outside and lit a cigarette.

I was so mad. He would ask me for money for bus fare and I would give it to him. I bought his stupid cigarettes at first, but after a little while I told him he no longer had a choice. He had to quit as we had no money for cigarettes. But he never seemed to run out. It irritated me so much that I was struggling and sacrificing everything for this life, for the relationship, for him. Whenever I brought up money or him finding a job, it was always an argument. He al-

CHAPTER 5

ways felt like I was nagging him and telling him he wasn't good enough when I was simply stressing about how much longer I could carry us. I would tell him he needed to spend less time with friends, just until he found a job, because his friends and "enjoying life" were his main priority.

As the arguments grew more frequent, I noticed that he had quite a temper. We hadn't argued before moving in together, so this was a new side of his. An ugly side. He would get so upset, as his level of anger rose, his face would redden. He'd clench his fists and hold his breath. He would then face the nearest wall and throw a hard and fast punch. He had done this three times by that point and there was a huge dent in the wall with two holes. I had moved the dresser in front of one of the holes to hide it. After punching the wall and maybe throwing some things, he would leave the house for hours. I would be left feeling empty and useless, cleaning up the mess.

We were behind on rent. My father had come knocking and when I answered, I told him we didn't have the money but that I'd pay him as soon as I got paid. When I was paid, all the money went towards bills and food and there honestly was no money left over for rent, so I decided to avoid my dad. When he came knocking, I would hide and pretend I wasn't home. I didn't answer his phone calls.

I was tired all the time. I was malnourished. My skin became greyer and greyer as time went on. I was unhappy and not so convincing at telling myself I was happy. I surprisingly missed my mother. I hadn't spoken to her since moving out. And although my father lived just downstairs, I hadn't spoken to him in months. My only comfort was my cat, but even she was being affected by the negativity as she spent more and more of her days outside. At night when Max and I would argue, she would hide in the bottom drawer of my dresser. I saw less and less of her over time.

My moments of intimacy with Max dwindled. We no longer cuddled before bed. We now slept on opposite sides. Some nights I would go to the bathroom and just cry. Sometimes I would cry in bed when I knew he was asleep. I was just so frustrated. I was supporting both of us and it was starting to weigh on me. A small part of me wished that he would wake up to my crying and cuddle me and realize how unhappy I was and make a change, but another part of me never wanted him to see me cry. I didn't want him to know just how miserable I was. I never needed to worry though; if he ever knew I was crying, he never let on. I felt very distant from the man I thought I loved, and it pained me. He, on the other hand, didn't notice or just didn't care—probably a bit of both. He wasn't home enough to see my dejection and when he was home, he was either sleeping or his mind would be elsewhere.

Our arguments became louder and more aggressive. He would kick the furniture and a few times, he picked up smaller items and throw them at the wall, breaking anything he thought might have value. The tenant next door had begun telling us that our arguing was disrupting his sleep. We often fought at night as I was working all day and he would be off with his friends. My father once knocked on our door so loud, I thought the glass might break. He came to tell us to shut up.

I was deeply troubled and hiding my sorrow wasn't easy. I tried to convince myself that it wasn't as bad as it seemed. That I was overreacting and needed to just let it go and then my life would be a little easier. Unfortunately, trying to convince myself didn't work, and I knew deep down that this was not how life was supposed to be.

CHAPTER 6

An Unkind Hand

Do you know what it's like to lie in bed next to a man you think you love, yet you feel so alone and so unloved? I do. It's a horrible feeling. It feels like being slowly swallowed by quicksand. There is no escape. No one is there to save you. You slowly drown until there is nothing left. All I wanted was to reach out to him and tell him I didn't want to argue. I wanted him to comfort me and hold me. I wanted him to be there for me when I cried myself to sleep and not just pretend to sleep.

I wanted all of that, but at the same time, I was mad and repulsed by his selfishness. And I was ashamed of wanting him to wrap me in his arms. I would lie there with nothing but these thoughts whirling around in my head, sobbing into my pillow so he couldn't hear. My loneliness consumed me.

Sometimes he would get out of bed and go sleep on the couch if I cried too loudly; then, I would really be all by myself, and it would make me cry more. I spent many nights like this. Eventually I would pass out from sheer exhaustion. In the morning when I would wake, I was accompanied by a painful headache reminding me once again of the agony I had endured.

I don't remember the argument or how it started. It was probably about work; most were about his lack thereof. We were in the bedroom yelling at each other when suddenly, out of the blue, he slapped me hard across the face. My jaw hit the floor. I couldn't believe what he had done—what had just occurred. Time froze and the sting of his hand against my face began to set in slowly. I put my hand on my face where he had hit me. My cheek was hot.

I looked at him in utter disbelief, and he stared back at me in what also seemed to be disbelief. He had never hit me before. I stepped back away from him, and he quickly stepped towards me and grabbed my arms—at first tightly, then they became gentle touches. He apologized profusely, over and over and said he would never ever lay a finger on me again. He wrapped me in his arms and told me I was shaking. He told me he loved me and that he would never want to hurt me in any way. We stood there for some time, me in his arms. He gently rubbed my back, soothing me almost like a baby.

That day, I learned what he was capable of, or so I thought. I was soon to find out that that wasn't even close to how bad things would get. I knew he had anger issues. He had punched a large hole into our bedroom wall—and also in his bedroom at his mother's house, which he had created when he had been angry with her. But he had never hit me before, and I never thought he would. Even drunk, I never thought he would do such a thing—but he was completely sober when he had hit me. That night, I slept on the bathroom floor. I didn't want to be near him.

The next morning, I snuck into the room while Max was sleeping and grabbed my clothes. I got dressed and headed to school. Max showed up a couple of hours later. From where I was sitting, I could see him looking around for me. But I wasn't in our regular spot. I was instead sitting with my girlfriends again, which was nice, but I think they knew something was up because I hadn't sat with them for some time now and I wasn't my usual chatty self that I always had been with them when we did sit together.

Max came over to me and asked me if we could go talk. I told him I was busy doing my work but that maybe afterwards I could take a break with him. He went to wait for me outside, catching up with all his old smoking buddies, I assumed. I made him wait what I thought was an acceptable time to take me seriously before heading outside. When I opened the door, I found him right where I thought he would be: in the smoker's pit.

I saw him, we made eye contact and I swiftly turned my heels and headed in the opposite direction. I headed towards the park I liked to walk in, and he followed quietly behind me. If he were a dog, he would have had his tail between his legs, touching his belly. He looked rather pathetic; his head was low and he had his hands in his pockets, quite different from the Max I had encountered the night before. I stopped when we reached a park bench and I sat down. He stood there seeming unsure as to what to do next. He paced as he apologized again for slapping me. He told me he didn't want me to leave him. It would break his heart and he couldn't live without me. He promised to never lay a hand on me again. He seemed remorseful about how he had behaved the night before.

CHAPTER 6

With crossed arms and legs, I told him that I did not tolerate that kind of behaviour and that I was not going to be in a violent relationship. I told him if he wanted to be with me, he needed to get a job right away and stop getting stupid drunk with his friends when he should be out job hunting. I was firm. I told him he wasn't allowed to spend money on alcohol at all and that he had to start contributing, otherwise I'd leave. He agreed to work harder at finding jobs and stop hanging out at his buddy's house all the time and drinking so much. We walked quietly back to school. I went back inside to finish my studies and he left.

I went to work after school, a nice break from the crazy twenty-four hours I had just had. Max called my cell a couple of times and I ignored it, which I never did. I stayed at work as late as I possibly could, offering my help to other people instead of just leaving when I was finished.

I wanted Max to sulk and feel really shitty about what he had done, so I stayed at work and hoped he would wait up for me like I had done for him time and time again. I caught the last bus home. When I was walking towards the house, I noticed the bedroom light was on. I figured he must have stayed up waiting. I climbed the stairs taking my time, opened the front door, tiptoed down the hallway and put my ear against the bedroom door.

What did I hear? Snoring. That jerk was soundly sleeping, not sulking. I opened the bedroom door and slammed it shut behind me, waking him up. "Oh, hey. You're home. I waited up, but I guess I fell asleep." *Bullshit*. I didn't even acknowledge him. I grabbed my pajamas and headed to the bathroom. I changed in the bathroom and brushed my teeth, my usual routine before bed. I contemplated sleeping on the bathroom floor, but the old, cold tile floor wasn't very appealing. I headed back to the bedroom and pulled the covers over me, noticing Max was naked. We often slept naked as we enjoyed a nice romp in the sheets late at night.

Once I got settled into bed, facing away from him, I felt him creep up behind me and put his arms around me. "Good night," he whispered quietly in my ear, "I love you." I would have pushed him away, but it had been ages since I felt any sort of comfort or love and I was craving some loving touches. And even though I felt as though this whole situation wasn't right anymore, deep down I still loved him, and I knew he loved me, too. I let him hold me and that's how we fell asleep.

The next few weeks were quite stressful. The memory of what had happened was still there, but Max was working harder to get a job. I stupidly bought him his own cell phone so that employers could call him. I was nervous as it was under my name since I had good credit, but I thought of the benefits for Max to have his own phone. We were down to our last dollars. I was going to the food bank to get food because I was too embarrassed to go to the grocery store after what had happened the last time I was there.

I would go to the food bank by myself. Each person was allowed two grocery bags of nonperishable foods—per week. I'd try to get Max to come with me so we could have more food, but he never wanted to go, so I was only able to get the two bags for us to share. The food didn't last long. He was a teenaged boy and he ate like one. Two bags of groceries would only last us two days.

Max finally got a job at a restaurant as a dishwasher. It didn't pay much, but I was so excited for him and for myself. It meant he was busy being proactive during the day, but he would still come home with beer sometimes and he could finally buy his own cigarettes, which didn't help us any. Occasionally, he would go to the dollar store alone, but usually the both of us went to buy food. It was a nice change because prior to that it felt like I was giving him an allowance, although I never knew what he spent it on. I no longer had to do that, which made me quite happy.

I was only spending maybe ten hours a week at school and working an awful lot. I was struggling. I felt the weight of the world on my shoulders. I was under a lot of stress, and I had begun suffering from major migraines. My friends tried to show their concern for me, but I didn't want it. I didn't want people pitying me. Maybe that's not what they were doing, but it felt like it, so I hid myself at school. I would sit in a little room all by myself where no one could bother me. I was starting to become a bit of a loner as I had blocked everyone out except Max, who didn't bother going to school anymore. He had pretty much dropped out.

Just being at school made me ill. I didn't like being there because I felt like everyone was watching me and secretly knew about my life. It made me paranoid. I felt out of place there; it was no longer my safe space.

I took ibuprofen for my migraines—that usually did the trick. One day, my head hurt so bad, I was dizzy, so I went home sick. The next day, I called in sick, and the next day as well. But I kept working because I had to. I worked extra and overtime. Soon enough, I was no longer going to school. I was working full time as well as a few other jobs on the side. I was a very busy person but all I could think about was how badly we needed the money. Most nights,

CHAPTER 6

I got home late and went straight to bed. I was so tired, I didn't even feel like eating. My life was work and sleep.

Max got fired from his job because of his temper and poor work ethic. He was furious when he came home that day. He was throwing things around the house. He started throwing these temper tantrums more frequently. He had no patience and no idea how to deal with stress or life in general, so he would take it out on the poor house. He would throw things, rip clothes and bed sheets and punch the walls. He managed to put another big dent in the wall, which I eventually covered with a poster. "You can't go punching the walls. This is our home and we have nowhere else to go. We can't afford anything and if we get kicked out, we'll be on the street," I yelled at him through tears. I didn't want to be in this violent house and I didn't want to be on the street. We had nowhere else to go and Max knew that. He mumbled that he hated the house before slamming the front door and disappearing for the night.

Even things that were not my fault, I was blamed for: I didn't make enough money, I didn't cook enough food—even the fact that he couldn't find a job was blamed on me. He blamed me for "picking fights and wrecking his day." He would say he couldn't go out and look for a job after the mood I had put him in, so he would end up going to his friend's house—spending the day getting high, drunk or both.

My poor cat didn't like the environment our house had become. She hid a lot when Max was around. She used to cuddle with us, but since the arguing got worse, she retreated into the bottom drawer of my dresser. Once things got really bad, she didn't even acknowledge Max. She didn't like him anymore. She would come out of her hidey-hole at night when I was alone. She would crawl up under the covers and cuddle with me and lick the tears off my face. She was very intuitive. She knew when I was sad, and she was always there for me. But when Max would come home, she'd go back in her hiding place. She knew he wasn't a good person.

In those days, the only socializing I did was at work. Luckily, I still loved my job. Being around the animals all day was my therapy, my break from the insane life that I led. My friends rarely called me and when they would ask how I was, I would give them some bullshit story about how Max and I were working hard and saving money and in general doing really well, which was, of course, all a lie.

One day during one of Max's regular temper tantrums, I was standing in the corner of the room out of reach of flying objects, and my father came up banging on our front door. Yelling at us to keep it down, he said: "I know you guys are home. I can hear stuff being thrown around. Come answer this door!" I wanted to run and answer the door, but Max read my mind. And before I knew it, Max's hands were tight around my throat.

"Don't you dare answer the door. Your father is not welcome in our home. He hates both of us. This has nothing to do with him anyways." He pushed me against the wall, still with a firm hold on my throat. "Don't you dare say anything." After a while of not hearing anything, I suspect my father gave up and went away because suddenly everything went quiet. All I could hear was Max's heavy breath and my heart in my throat, on which his hands were still grasped. "This is your fault," he said in a low voice, "If only you would stop nagging me about not having a job, or my smoking and the occasional drink I have with my friends."

When I tried to speak, he would tighten his grip on my throat. I studied his face, my eyes pleading with him to let go of me, but all I saw looking back was a monster. Max was no longer in there. Someone or something else was inside him, something evil and mean. He gave another tight squeeze and then let go of my throat as quickly as he had grabbed it. His chest was puffing as if he had just had a strenuous workout.

He took a step back and a hard swing, this time hitting my jaw. It hurt like hell. I never saw it coming. It happened so fast, I had no time to react. I was bewildered and in so much pain. Opening my mouth to flex my jaw was excruciating. That was now the second time he had hit me. He went and sat on the bed. I leaned against the wall, my legs giving out from under me, and I slid down to the floor in a heap. My mind was spinning about my life. *Is this how my life is going to be from now on? Is it always going to be like this? Destruction and abuse?*

Max was on the bed cradling his head in his hands, shaking his head and ruffling his hair. The monster I was getting to know had several faces: the evil one, the pathetic one, the nice one and the one that made you want to pick him up and cradle him. He looked at me with his puppy eyes and softly said, "Why do you make me do this to you? Why do you make me so angry when you know what I'll do? I don't want to hurt you, but you make me so angry, and I can't control myself. Why, Babe? Why do you do it?" He put his head back in his hands.

Is it me causing this, making him like this? Is it my fault? I began to consider the idea that maybe I was just getting what I deserved. I actually made myself believe that it was all my doing, as if I had the power to turn him into the monster that I hated. I got up and went to the bathroom. I looked at my reflection in the mirror. I was gaunt, colourless, dull. I put some cold water on my face as I pondered the notion that I was the problem and the reason for unleashing this demon he had become. I went to the kitchen and grabbed an ice pack from the freezer. I sat down at the table holding the ice pack to my jaw and I took three extra strength ibuprofens. I sat there, my mind reeling.

I wanted to leave, but I didn't have anywhere to go. I sat there for fifteen minutes, which felt like longer, before I finally moved. I put the ice pack back in the freezer and walked down the hallway to the bedroom. Max was still sitting on the bed, but now his elbows were on his knees, and he was looking out the window, his hands tightly grasped together. I stood by the dresser, close to the doorway. "Why do you let me do it?" he asked, looking at me vulnerably, as if waiting for my permission to breathe. "Why? I love you and I never want to hurt you. But you make me so angry and I lose control. I know it's not good, but I can't help it."

He looked down at the floor and shook his head. He stood up and walked over to me. He made a gesture to lift his hand and I flinched until his hand rested gently on my cheek. "I don't want that. I don't want you flinching every time I reach to touch you. I love you. I never want to hurt you. I am so sorry." Then he gently grabbed my shoulders and said, "I don't want to hurt you. So don't let me. Next time, punch me."

I couldn't believe what I was hearing. He was giving me permission to hit him if he ever tried to hit me again. "Really?" I said, unsure of what exactly he was saying. "You're going to let me hit you?" He nodded and gave me a hug. I thought to myself, *Am I capable of hitting someone I love?* I didn't really know what to say. I had never hit anyone in my life, and I was hoping there would be less hitting, not more.

CHAPTER 7

Manipulated and Alone

We had an old-style TV with the big back on it. Max found it one night on one of his drunken escapades. It was sitting on the side of the road. It was right when flat screens were coming out, so the big clunky ones were now out of style and up for grabs. The day after it had been spotted, we went with a buddy of his and the two boys carried this heavy large awkward object to the house and up the narrow stairs. It was insanely heavy, but we managed somehow to lift it up onto the dresser. We didn't have cable, but Max liked to play his video games, so that's what it was mainly used for. One day during another terrible temper tantrum, he turned into the Incredible Hulk, picked up this massive television and attempted to hurl it in my direction.

Lucky for me, the TV couldn't fly very far—thank God—but Max could, and he was right behind the TV. Before I knew it, I threw my hands up to protect my face and he punched me hard right in the gut. I could feel the air from my body deflate with the blow. My arms fell to cover my stomach as he was making a fist for punch number two, headed for my face. "Don't you dare, Max. I'm warning you. Remember what you told me last time. I'll hit you right back," I said, trying to sound confident as it had slowed him down a little bit, but he was still in monster mode. He saw this as a challenge.

"Go ahead," he said with a creepy smirk on his face. "But make it count," he added.

I froze. I didn't know what to do. He was standing there with his arms down, unguarded, waiting for me to hit him. I had never punched anyone before, so I was worried that it wouldn't be powerful enough to stop him.

I'm not a fighter. I don't want to hurt people; that's not my thing. Even after everything, I didn't want to hit him, but I knew I had to. I was going to punch him in the nose. I made a fist, lifted my arm, and attempted to aim. But as soon as my hand left my side, I felt it lose strength. Suddenly, everything went black.

I woke up; I don't know how long after. I was lying on the bedroom floor alone with a pounding migraine. *Did I punch him?* I wasn't sure what had happened. I wasn't sure if I even threw a punch. I don't know if I hit him and then he hit me or even if he let me hit him. I couldn't remember anything; I still don't, but that's probably for the better.

The front door was wide open. All the doors were, so I assumed that he had stormed out afterwards. I lay there and felt a soft nuzzle under my neck. My sweet, sweet cat was there. Comforting me like she always did. I took five extra strength ibuprofens and carried my cat to bed to cuddle and sleep. I was so exhausted, I felt like I could sleep forever.

Max didn't come home until early the following morning. I don't know if it was his presence that awoke me or my cat going back into her hiding place, but I woke up. I lay there super still, pretending to be asleep. He changed, got into bed and fell asleep quickly.

I never threw another punch. I had learnt the hard way never to do that again.

It's hard to recall every hit I was at the receiving end of. It was becoming a frequent thing in my life. Some weeks it was daily, others it was maybe twice a week. A week might have gone by without a hit from him. Time just kept moving and life kept going and so did we. We were going through the motions. I felt dead inside. I was a zombie—a walking, working zombie. Slaps became punches. If I fell to the ground, I would get kicked. I had several objects thrown at me. I was living in hell; it was my new "normal."

I would regularly seem to say or do something wrong that would upset Max and cause him to get violent with me. He would grab my arms and hold them behind my back in an extremely uncomfortable position while he would spit in my face and call me horrendous names. Sometimes it was in the morning while I was getting ready for work that he would lose it, or it would happen when I got home late from work. He was completely unpredictable. I never knew when it was going to happen next. I lived day by day waiting, knowing it was coming.

Max had me convinced that it was all my doing, that it was my fault why he got so angry and would hurt me, especially since I had known he had anger issues. I would spend all day thinking, *If only I hadn't said this*, or *If only I had done that differently.* I was constantly questioning and doubting myself. Max had killed my self-esteem and my confidence.

I had put so much time and effort into the relationship, I didn't want to throw it all away; I felt that it would make me a failure if I did. When we were arguing and he was yelling at me, he would tell me that I was an unlovable person and that only he was and ever would be capable of loving someone like me. He made me believe that I was worthless and that no one else would love me, and I didn't want to be alone.

I was always at home if I wasn't at work or out with Max because that was what he expected of me. I was always cautious around Max. I had to tiptoe around him all the time so that I wouldn't upset him and possibly cause another tantrum. I worked very hard at trying not to rock the boat in even the slightest way, otherwise all hell would break loose.

I had dropped out of school, and there was rarely a moment that Max was not at my side. I used to plan parties and be more social, but now I made no effort at all to stay in touch with my friends, let alone hang out with them. My friends had watched me as I turned from a bubbly, social, talkative and happy person to this now shell of a woman. I was now anti-social, withdrawn from everything and everyone. I had become like a shadow in the corner.

One of my closest girlfriends was concerned for me. She had noticed a drastic change in my behaviour as well as in my appearance. One day, she decided to give me an ultimatum. Either I broke up with Max and we would remain friends, or I stayed with Max and she would no longer be my friend. She told me that it was too hard for her to watch me turn into something I wasn't and to let myself be miserable. She knew something wasn't right although she didn't know what it exactly was.

I had neglected my friends. I had pretty much disowned my parents. I isolated myself and I wouldn't let the outside world in. And now, the door to the outside world was closing behind me. Before, it had been open, with me standing at the door looking outside; now, it was closing on my face.

I was confused. I didn't know what I had done to deserve being abandoned by my best friend. I told her that there was no reason for this and that I needed her as a friend but that Max also needed me. I told her I wasn't going to accept the ultimatum, so she left. Once she graduated, not long after the ultimatum, she moved away and I didn't speak to her for years. The day she walked out of my life I will never forget. She took a piece of me with her: hope. The only thing I had a little of was hope that the hell I was living in would end.

CHAPTER 7

I lost my best friend, the only friend I had left in the world. I wasn't about to let the only thing I had in my life, the only person who still loved me, go away, so I held on to Max tighter like my life depended on it. I decided I would be a better girlfriend and devote myself entirely to Max and making him happy. Because once again, I didn't want to be alone. I thought if I could just be better that he would love me better.

My world once again shrank and I felt as though I lived in a fishbowl—watching the outside world while swimming around in circles. My life consisted of work and trying to make the most out of my relationship with Max. With my best friend gone and no one else to turn to, I found myself once again alone, with only Max in my corner—a very dark and gloomy corner to be in.

I remember the first time I realized there were bruises all over my body. I had distinct fingerprint marks on my arms from where Max had grabbed me, multiple times. I also had spotted marks around my neck. Bruises were popping up all over—mostly on my ribs and legs from being kicked. Most of them were covered, especially in the winter. In the summer, I loved to wear tank tops and shorts, but I could no longer do that.

After that punch to the jaw, Max learned quickly that he shouldn't aim for my eyes or nose as that would show bruising and because even really well done makeup couldn't cover everything up. Believe me, I tried.

He had slapped me a few times, but when he was enraged and really wanted to hurt me, he would throw a nasty punch usually aimed at my jaw and cheek. It always left a sting and my face would be red and sore. After I put cold water and ice on my face, the redness would go away.

On most days that he would beat me, I wouldn't leave the house—unless I had to work. I couldn't miss work. I would dress in long shirts and pants—even during the hot summer months. I would cover my face in makeup, fake a smile and head out.

There were a couple of days that I really was unable to work. and those days I would lie in bed all day and sleep as my body was exhausted from the life I was living. I covered the bruises not only to prevent others from seeing them but also to hide them from myself. They were cold, hurtful reminders of the things that had been done. Things that sometimes I couldn't remember. I woke up alone on the floor often.

I'd sooner or later discover a bruise in the shower or while getting dressed. I used to point them out to Max and I would tell him that one day someone was going to suspect something. He never seemed to worry about it. He felt

CHAPTER 7

so confident in his little house with his protective shield around it. Eventually I stopped showing him my bruises.

One day, I was closing at work when my supervisor asked me to come to her office upon finishing. I nodded yes composedly, but my head was spiraling with possibilities as to what she could possibly want to talk to me about.

Anticipation hung in the air as I finished up the last-minute things and checked to make sure everything was ready for the night shift person. I had mentioned to several people that I wanted to become the veterinarian's assistant as the current one was going to be leaving and the position was still up for grabs.

I knocked on my supervisor's slightly open door. "Come in," she said in a calm, matter-of-fact way, "Have a seat." I walked into the office feeling confident yet nervous. I had been working extremely hard and offering more help in the Trauma unit when I was finished with my duties. I had stayed late when asked, came in on days off, and worked overtime. I was really hoping I was going to get the job.

She pointed to the chair across from her. She asked me how work was going, whether I still enjoyed it, and if I was getting along with everyone. I was a bit surprised at these questions. Having been there for over a year and never having had a problem, I assured her that I thought I was doing well and hadn't heard otherwise. I made sure she knew how much I loved the job and what it meant to me. She looked at me as if pondering what to say next.

"You don't seem as happy as you say you are. Even some of the other girls are saying you aren't the happy-go-lucky girl we once knew and originally hired to work here," she said.

I looked at my hands wrapped together tightly in my lap. "The girls say you seem depressed and as though you aren't happy here anymore. And that makes it less fun for them to work with you," she added, using words that burned. I wasn't expecting this at all. I knew I wasn't the same person, but I didn't know what to say. How do you tell your boss, "*Oh, I'm sorry. My boyfriend decided to beat me today before work, but I'll try harder tomorrow not to piss him off so he doesn't beat me again*"?

I had no explanation for her. I told her I was sorry and that I would try harder. "Today was your last shift," she said very coldly, "We appreciate the work you've done, but I don't see you belonging in this environment anymore. Go take some time off—for yourself."

Her words were a slap in the face. She stood up to open the door and gave a small nod. I walked out of the office and waved goodbye to the front staff who were completely unaware of what had just happened. I felt as though I myself was unaware of what had just happened. I waved to them as if I would see them the next day, but I would never walk through those doors again.

Warm tears started to build and then run down my cheeks. Work was the last place I had where I was safe and happy. I wiped my face when the bus pulled up. I took one last look at the clinic before turning away and getting on the bus. I left the clinic and all the good memories behind. Another door had slammed in my face.

It was true I had become depressed. I knew I wasn't a bundle of joy. But I still worked hard, which didn't end up counting for anything.

When I got home, I had a migraine from crying and trying not to cry on the bus all at the same time. I was still in shock from what happened, so I just got ready for bed. I took a few ibuprofens to help me sleep and cuddled under the blankets. The next morning, I woke up with another migraine. I was in so much pain, even the sun hurt my eyes. It felt like a hangover after a night of mixing liquors. I took more ibuprofen and went back to bed, putting my head under the covers to keep the light out. I slept all day.

I had been developing migraines from the stress and everything else going on, so I always kept a bottle of ibuprofen nearby. Now it seemed I was going through them quicker than before.

Now that I was not working, Max insisted I go everywhere with him and do everything with him. In the mornings, he'd wake up and tell me that so-and-so had bought a new game or a new movie to watch. I didn't feel forced to go to his friend's houses at the time, but it was better than being alone all day, and often when we were at his friend's homes, we were fed, so it was also one less meal I had to scrounge.

Our days consisted mainly of sitting on a couch at one of his many friends' houses. We would play cards and smoke weed, which helped my headaches, but I always had my ibuprofen in my purse just in case. Our days were filled with empty errands. We would go visit one friend at work, then we'd go for a walk to the beach so he and his buddy could drink beer. We would spend hours, sometimes weekends, just hanging out at his friends' houses. There were many nights we didn't go home. And my brain and body were numb to it all. My new normal was wearisome as I waited for my ventriloquist to come along and tell me what to do.

One day, Max and I were on the bus with a buddy of his and his girlfriend as we always seemed to travel with an entourage. We were going downtown. Max and I were arguing as usual but trying to keep it low-key because we were in public. Max was being verbally cruel, so I decided I wasn't going to sit next to him on the bus. I moved seats so my back was towards him and his friends.

Max then started whispering mean things in my ear. I don't distinctly remember what he said but I chose to ignore him, and as a result, he grabbed tiny strands of my hair and ripped them out.

"Stop that, Max!" I turned around and scowled at him as he and his friend laughed. It was like a game to him. He did it again and again. And then his friend did it. I couldn't believe it. My boyfriend felt like he could treat me like absolute garbage and now his friends thought they could, too. I stood up and got off the bus as soon as the doors opened. I walked home.

Max never went after me to apologize. I walked for probably half an hour or so. I didn't know what to do. I didn't want to go home in case Max was there, but I also had nowhere else to go and I knew that the chances of Max being home were quite slim, so I continued to walk, heading for home. When I arrived, I curled up under the sheets and sobbed into my pillow. I felt helpless. I didn't want to live like this. The world was a brutal and hurtful place. I didn't want to be a part of it anymore. I reached for my bag and pulled out my ibuprofen. I counted them in my hand as I wondered how many pills it would take to overdose. I took a handful and went to bed.

CHAPTER 8

Fighting for Control

I awoke the next morning, still alive but with a bad stomachache as a reminder of what I had done the night before. I lay in bed all day. When Max came home, he noticed the almost empty bottle of pills next to the bed. "Another migraine?"

I nodded, not looking at him.

"You've been taking more and more of these lately. You've almost finished the bottle." That was all he said before heading into the kitchen.

He was right. I was taking a lot and I never went anywhere without them. They were my magical remedy for everything.

I remember the first time I ever took an ibuprofen just as vividly as one would remember their first time having sex. I was at a girlfriend's house, and I can't remember exactly why, but I had a headache, so my friend then offered me a pill. She poured it out of the bottle and handed it to me.

I remember how it felt. It was small and soft. It was a nice red colour. When I put it in my mouth, the coating tasted like sugar. It was sweet. I wanted to let it just melt on my tongue, but my friend handed me a glass of water, so instead I got to feel it slide down my throat ever so smoothly.

The result was instantaneous. It was truly magical. After that, I went out and bought myself some.

The pills were great. I had a bottle in the bedroom, in the bathroom and in my purse. They seemed to fix every problem I had. I took them for both pain relief and to feel numb. They cured my migraines and helped me sleep better. For any reason I could think of, I would take one or two. It was becoming a daily thing for me to take my pills. I would take them after beatings and in between. I thought they would help my body recover more quickly. I would take them to desensitize my body so I could go on another day living in my chaotic yet dull environment. There was no middle ground anymore. It was either absolute chaos or being absolutely stoned.

CHAPTER 8

One day, Max and I were sitting at a food court in the mall downtown. I had my usual migraine, so I reached into my purse and grabbed my bottle of magic pills. I popped three without even thinking about it and then put my bottle back in my purse. Max gave me an angry look and said, "You sure are taking a lot of those. I rarely see you without that bottle nearby." I simply shrugged. *It's not any of his business*, I thought to myself.

"I don't want you taking those anymore. They aren't good for you and you're taking too many. Actually, give me that bottle," he demanded.

"No," I answered firmly and a little louder than I had intended. I looked around to see if anyone was watching us. Luckily, food courts are quite noisy anyway, so no one was watching us.

"Fine then," he answered matter-of-factly.

He had a safety pin that was holding his sweater's sleeve together. He removed it from his sweater and pointed it at me. "You see this?" he said before rolling down his sleeve. He then proceeded to drag the pin across his wrist.

Again, I looked around, but no one was watching. A red line formed with a tinge of blood. I was utterly shocked and disgusted at what I had just witnessed, and in a public food court of all places.

"Every time you take one of your stupid pills, I'm going to do this to myself. You think you can hurt yourself? Well, I can hurt myself too." I was speechless.

"I love you and those pills are not doing you any good." He hugged me and whispered in my ear that he cared about me too much to lose me. I agreed to stop. I didn't want him slitting his wrists. My naivete told me that he loved me. He didn't want me hurting myself because it hurt him, so he was willing to hurt himself if it meant I would stop hurting myself.

He wrapped his wrist tightly in his sleeve and we left the food court hand in hand.

After that, nothing was said again about the pills. To his knowledge, I had flushed them all down the toilet, but like most men, he would never go in my purse, so I kept my bottle there.

I didn't want to lie to him, but I couldn't have him cutting himself and I couldn't go without my wonderful magical pills. They were the only thing keeping me afloat. I don't know if I was addicted to them, but I knew I didn't want to be without them. So, from then on, I was stealthy. I would wait for Max to leave the house or I would go to the bathroom to take my pills. I needed them to take the edge off, and they did just that.

Soon after the incident at the mall, we finally got what

was coming to us. One day, we came home to a note on our door stating that we were being evicted. We had until the following Monday to get out. Since my father was the landlord, there was no disputing the letter or even discussing it. In the note, he mentioned that we fought too much and that he was concerned about all the noise that sounded like us breaking things.

There were a lot of holes in the walls I really didn't want my father to see before moving out, so I went to the paint store and bought some plaster and paint and Max and I repaired the holes and dents. Afterwards, the place looked somewhat decent again. We didn't own much, so moving wouldn't be too hard. We'd leave the furniture, and the rest of our stuff could fit in suitcases.

I called my mother, whom I hadn't spoken to for over a year. I asked her if she could take my cat. I told her we had gotten evicted. She had no idea where we even lived. I told her the new place we were moving to didn't allow pets. She said she would take the cat. I was very saddened to have to give up my one and only true friend and possibly the only thing on the planet that cared for me. But this was only going to be temporary—only until we could find a place that allowed cats. In the meantime, we didn't have anywhere to go.

I had lied to my mum about the new place. There was no new place. We slept on Max's friends' couches, switching it up every so often so as to not wear out our welcome. I would try to make myself useful and help around the house to show appreciation to our hosts. It kept me busy—and out of Max's way. Luckily during this time, life was a party to him. He was with his buddies 24/7. We never knew where our next meal was going to come from or whose couch we'd be on the next night.

We had taken advantage of all his friends' couches, and having overstayed them, we had to spend a few nights outside. It wasn't horrible, but I don't recommend it either. We had to use outhouses in the park. Being in the park, I realized how many other people lived there, like us, and I didn't like that at all.

I couldn't accept the fact that we were homeless. I didn't want to end up like this. I explained to Max how I felt and how we weren't set up to live outdoors. So, one day, he finally mustered up the strength to call his mother.

He, like myself at this point, had a rocky relationship with his mother—but way worse than mine with my mother. He used to steal her cigarettes and alcohol and, of course, punch holes in her walls, so she wasn't really keen on having the two of us staying at her place. But we

CHAPTER 8

thought we'd give it a try since we had nowhere else to go. She told us we could go over the following day. That night, we slept under the stars again, and the next morning, we headed to see Max's mother.

She welcomed us in but, of course, wasn't thrilled about seeing us. She wasn't pleased about the situation, but we told her we were desperate and would do anything as we had nowhere else to go.

We sat down with Max's mum and his sister Amber at the dinner table and Max's mum pulled out a contract for each of us to sign. "I've written up this contract, and you are not welcome to live here unless you abide by the rules in this contract. Is that understood?" she said firmly.

Max and I nodded.

We went over the contract. There were a few basic house chores we had to do plus a few extra things like weeding the garden and painting the fence. Mostly it was housework. Keeping the house clean, not being pigs—the usual. And of course, if we broke or damaged anything, we would have to fix it or pay to have it fixed.

She stared coldly into Max's eyes. "If you punch any holes anywhere in this house, you are both out and you will never be allowed back."

"Yes, mum," he said sincerely, looking down at his lap.

After going over the contract, the three of us signed it and that was it. We were allowed to move in. Thank God. No more couchsurfing or living in the park. That was all in the past now. It didn't take us long to move in and get settled. Like I mentioned earlier, we really didn't have a lot of stuff. The house was a little cramped with both his mum and his sister living there, but we made it work.

During the day, his mum went to work and Amber was in school. At first, we worked hard to honour the terms of the contract. I would weed the garden while Max painted the fence. Inside, he would clean the kitchen and I would do the bathrooms. He would take the garbage out at night. We had a system and so far, it had worked. I hung out with Amber sometimes when she would get home from school. She was a nice kid and I saw her as a little sister. We grew to be quite close, us girls.

Max would fight with his mum a bit, which wasn't good, but I was happy for the break on my end. I was happy he had someone else to pick on, though he was never violent with her. She was a tough woman. She would have killed him if he had tried anything on her. I suppose he saw me as a weak little thing he could do with what he chose.

CHAPTER 8

After maybe two weeks, we started fighting when no one else was home. And he would always start with stupid things like, "We moved out so we wouldn't have to do all this crap," and I would explain to him how we had signed an agreement with his mum, so unless he wanted to be homeless again—which I didn't want—he would have to follow the rules in the contract.

The house was in a complex and Max's mother told us that the neighbours had heard Max and I arguing. It felt a little stifling and I felt I always had to be on my best behaviour, not only to not upset Max but also because of the close neighbours.

I ended up doing a lot of his chores as well as my own. Sometimes, he was gone and I'd have the house all to myself. I would put some fast-paced dance music on, not too loud but loud enough. I'd wash the dishes and put them away, do the laundry, clean the kitchen and the bathrooms. His mum would come home and be so happy with how clean the house looked. I never told her I did it all, but I think she suspected it. Sometimes she would get home and Max wasn't there, so she must have known. At least she was happy. She was free to do some work on the computer and I would watch a movie until dinner or Max arrived, whichever came first.

One night, I was busy cleaning and Max was out gallivanting with his friends doing whatever the hell it was that they did, and his mother and sister came home early because his sister had been sent to the principal's office. Max's mother was obviously upset with Amber and told her to go upstairs and put her backpack away. She then sat at her computer.

I wasn't expecting their arrival for a couple more hours, so I was in shorts and a tank top, my cleaning clothes. I wasn't sure what to do. I felt awkward and exposed. I thought I should go to the bedroom and wait for Max to come home, but I decided to first finish cleaning the bathroom.

I was at the bottom of the stairs about to climb up to go to the bedroom when his mother turned around to talk to me. At that same moment, Amber came back downstairs. She sat near me and I noticed her staring at my arms.

"What's this?" She looked at me, grabbed my arm and pointed out my bruises. I looked at my arm where his sister was holding me, and I gasped. Bruises, finger mark bruises, clear as day. Anyone with half a brain would have known that. Lucky for me, she was young.

"Does my brother beat you?" she said jokingly. His mother looked at me when she said that, her eyes searching my face for a response; she waited for it calmly as she sat in her chair.

"Of course not," I said, trying to laugh a little, "I don't know how I got those. I never noticed them. But I bruise easily. It could be from anything. It could be from carrying the heavy laundry basket or something silly like that." I tried to sound surprised. His mother gave me one more quick glance before deciding to believe my story and went back to her computer work. I think she may have had her suspicions, but she never said anything.

His sister headed then for the kitchen as it was her night to make dinner. That was the first time that anyone had ever seen a bruise on me or said anything, even just as a joke. I quickly ran upstairs to change and hid in the bedroom for the rest of the day. I was somewhat shaken from the whole encounter. They could have found out my secret. *What would Max do to me then?* Also, they were his family, so they might not have even believed me if I had told them. I knew I had to be more careful. No one could see me like that anymore. No one could know my dark secret.

I did have a close call one other time. Sometimes people just don't see—or don't want to see—what's right in front of their face. One day, I went to visit Max's friend

Rick at work, without Max. Rick was an old friend of Max's whom we visited frequently at his workplace downtown. I had just spent several days hiding from the world in the house recovering, but this day I was feeling better and wanting a friend, so I went out.

I had arrived right on time for his break. I said hello and we hugged as we always did. He said he hadn't seen me for a while and that we could head out once he grabbed his coat. Before turning around, he scanned me up and down and said, "Are you okay?" He sounded concerned, "Seriously, you look like someone whose husband beats them."

I was shocked and just for a second, I couldn't breathe. All I could do was shrug. All I could think to say was how the dollar store food didn't help and that I was working long hours at the clinic. I hadn't told anyone I was fired because I was totally embarrassed and ashamed.

This friend knew a lot about Max and I and our relationship, but of course not everything. We would often ask him for advice as he was a few years older than us and we both respected him very much. I visited him alone often when I had nothing else to do. I think he may have suspected that something was going on, but being a friend to us both, he probably didn't want to see it or couldn't imagine his friend doing that.

CHAPTER 8

Nothing else was said about it. We went outside, smoked a joint, talked a bit and then he headed back to work. I headed home. That was the last time I went to go see him alone, which was sad because he was the one friend of Max's I actually liked and respected.

That comment resonated with me. I used to take pride in what I wore and how I looked, but these things were becoming less important, and obviously, it was showing. It was clear that if I was going to be out in public since I couldn't hide in the house forever, I would have to try harder to look better. I couldn't have people knowing my secret. If Max had been with me when our friend did that, I probably would have gotten beaten up later at home for it. I would have to be more careful.

There was no such thing as being too careful. I had to develop a new persona. I thought of myself as a celebrity who led a miserable life but, being in the limelight, had no choice but to appear well put-together, confident and fierce. I had already started to practice being someone else in everyone else's eyes. It wasn't easy, though. It was easier to stay home, so more often than not, I did just that.

CHAPTER 9

From Bad to Worse

Since all his children had left home by then, my father planned to travel the globe during the Christmas season of 2008. He asked me if I would dogsit while he was away for three months. The dog had been our family dog for years before I moved out of the house. I loved this dog, such a sweet dog. So, of course, I happily agreed.

My father and I met up. It had been a while since I had seen him, let alone walked in his house, the house I grew up in. He gave me the basic rundown, instructions and all that stuff, and then he told me that I could stay under one condition, only one: Max was not welcome in or near the house. I was to dogsit— not Max. I thought about how I was going to work my way around this. I knew Max wouldn't like it. I promised my dad Max would not come into or near the house. This was another lie.

My dad was due to leave the following week, so the days that followed consisted of packing. I didn't own much, but I managed to pack just enough clothes so I didn't have to do laundry all the time. I spoke to Max about my father's instructions and his one condition.

Max, of course, was furious. He threw a tantrum and was yelling profanities about my father and then came to the conclusion that I was not allowed to stay at my father's house. I told him I had to. I wasn't going to let his dog starve and I wasn't going to take the bus twice a day every day to go feed the dog and then come back. We didn't have the money for that.

I told him it would be a good opportunity to give each other space. I would have a roof over my head and free meals as my father was a bit of a hoarder and had a huge deep freezer full of food, which was a huge stress reliever for me. I told Max as a compromise that he was allowed to come over and visit and we could hang out and eat dinner together some nights, but that he was not allowed to stay the night. He did not like the arrangement, but he agreed

CHAPTER 9

since it meant he could stay out late with his friends. I moved into my father's house and Max stayed at his mother's house.

The first few days at my dad's house I spent tidying and cleaning. I had nothing better to do. I cleaned the linens, made the beds and put clothes away or to be washed. I cleaned the kitchen as well as the bathroom. My father was a hard-working single man, seldom at home, so his housekeeping skills had long been forgotten. I would spend a couple of hours cleaning and then I would hop on my bike for a ten-minute ride to the beach with the dog. There was an area for the dogs to run loose and play. My dad's dog loved it. He was a very fit dog and he would just run and run, ears flapping and all.

We'd then go down to the water. He loved to play in the water, but for some silly reason, he wouldn't swim. I would throw sticks at the waves and he would look at me like *That's too far. I don't swim.* We would climb rocks, walk on logs and play for hours. It was such a nice break from my life. I absolutely loved going to the beach with the dog. I started to feel a little bit like my old self again. The change of pace was invigorating.

But when I arrived back at the house, I found Max sitting on the front steps waiting for me. "It's a shame you didn't come earlier. You could have joined us at the beach," I said out of breath. But, in truth, I was happy he didn't come with us. It wouldn't have been as much fun. "Maybe next time," he replied, giving the dog a pat. We hadn't seen each other in a couple of days, but it felt longer than that. He was in a good mood, which was nice. With us living apart, our relationship went a little more smoothly. We weren't arguing as much because when he'd get upset, he would just leave. He was behaving more like his old self.

I was happy for a bit of a break, but soon after that, I was only ever by myself when I was in the bathroom. Once he had spent the night after a late night of intimacy, he pretty much moved in.

I didn't want to take the risk of asking him to leave so I figured that as long as he wasn't causing trouble, it would be okay. Soon, I was doing his laundry with mine and we were eating together at dinner. But then some nights he would go gallivanting with his friends and he wouldn't come home. Sometimes he'd disappear for nights at a time. Those nights, I felt lonely because I had gotten used to having the man I had fallen in love with back. I was actually enjoying being with him again.

After maybe two weeks of this lovely blissful life, we started arguing again. At first, it was small things: he

CHAPTER 9

didn't want to discuss something that was important, or he hadn't taken the garbage out, or I had cooked dinner for us and he had just decided he was going to a friend's house and he'd probably eat there—silly things like that. But he always escalated things with his temper and unwillingness to calm down and work through problems. He started punching the walls, slamming doors and throwing things at me again.

Storming out of the kitchen, Max slammed the door behind him—a beautiful French glass door with a wooden frame—and several of the glass panes smashed into several pieces. Glass flew everywhere. The floor was covered in shards of glass. He didn't even bother to turn around and look at the damage he had caused or even offer to clean it up. He just kept walking straight out the front door, slamming it too. Thankfully, it was made of solid wood. I was left, once again, to clean up the mess. I carefully swept the floor in tears. I didn't know what to do. How was I going to explain this to my father? He would know that Max had been in here. I couldn't blame it on the dog. I had no idea how to get it fixed and I didn't have any money to fix it even if I wanted to. So, after I cleaned up the glass and took out the garbage, I sat on the sofa and just stared at the half-glass door.

A few days later, Max was out of smokes and we had no money for more. He was suffering withdrawals big time and it was unbearable.

I was cooking dinner when he started yelling and screaming. He was upset because he couldn't find something. He was rummaging through the kitchen cupboards and drawers. I don't remember what he was looking for, but he couldn't find what he needed. I remember he was holding a knife in his hands, but I didn't think much of it as he had never threatened me with an object or weapon before. So, I continued my cooking and let him rant.

He caught me taking a glance at him to see exactly what it was he was doing. I offered to help him find whatever it was he was looking for. He glared into my eyes, and his were black.

The monster was back. He looked down at his hand holding the knife. My eyes followed his. I shivered, nervous and scared, and for some sick reason, it made him smirk. He brought his hand with the knife up to my belly, slowly up my chest and then pointed right at my throat. He gently laid the side of the knife against my neck.

I froze like a statue. All I could think was *Is he going to slit my throat? What is happening here? We've been better*

CHAPTER 9

lately. I had been hoping all the violence was behind us, but I was wrong.

I could hear the wheels in his head turning and I was absolutely terrified to know what he was thinking. After what felt like forever, he slowly lowered his hand. He put the knife on the counter with the blade facing me and he went back to looking for this thing that seemed to possess him. I hurriedly walked to the bathroom and closed the door behind me and locked it. I didn't realize I had been holding my breath. I gasped and fell to the ground, crying and shaking with fear. I couldn't believe what he had just done. Now he was going to threaten me with knives. I cried for a bit and then searched the cabinets in the bathroom. I knew my dad probably had some ibuprofen around somewhere.

I found the bottle at the back of the cabinet, in a nice little hiding spot. I took a few pills and then ever so quietly and gently, so as not to shake it and rouse Max, I slipped the bottle back into the spot where I had found it. I slowly opened the bathroom door and peeked out, but I couldn't see him. I waited to hear him shuffling about or cursing. Nothing. I tiptoed out to the kitchen. No sign of him. I called out his name and there was no answer. He had left, with the front door wide open as usual. The doors were always either left open or slammed shut.

I locked the front door and went back to the kitchen. Dinner was finished cooking. I turned off all the elements and went to lie down in the bedroom. I soon fell asleep.

The next morning, I awoke abruptly. I wasn't sure what woke me until I heard it again. It was a loud knock on the side door of the bedroom leading outside. Max was standing on the porch, banging on the door and calling out my name. I lay there, still and quiet, wishing he would just go away. But after the four times he called my name, I knew he wouldn't leave and that I'd have to get up.

I slowly got out of bed. It was 8 a.m.—unusually early for him. I slowly unlocked and opened the door, peering out. I saw Max and a friend of his standing on the porch. "Hey, Baby," he said casually, as if the night before had never happened. He smiled sweetly at me, "I'm here to get a change of clothes. My friend's workplace needs a few extra hands today, so I'm going to go make some money."

"Okay," I answered awkwardly. I wasn't sure what he was up to, and I could only imagine what he was actually going to do that day, but I could care less. I opened the door. He came in and quickly changed into clean clothes. On his way out, he told me he'd be home late, gave me a quick kiss on the cheek and closed the door behind him, which I locked before going back to bed.

CHAPTER 9

Before this point in our relationship, I understood mentally that Max was cruel and vindictive, but my heart still wanted to believe in him. We were both big parts of each other's lives. I still had hope that once he was stable in life, he would once again become the man I had fallen in love with. I saw glimpses of the man I had fallen for when he was happy, but his anger could be triggered by anything and then the dark monster within would take over.

My brain and heart were in a constant dance. I wasn't sure if I wanted it to end. But after this event, my heart was starting to waver. I knew that I no longer wanted to be in the relationship, but I didn't know how to get out of it—safely. I knew that if I locked him out of the house, he wouldn't hesitate to break a window or two to get inside. I was on a rocky roller coaster ride, and I couldn't get off of it. Apparently, this ride wasn't over yet and I was starting to wonder—and dread—what the end of the ride would look like.

I no longer knew how to act around Max. I was always careful. I didn't want to say or do the wrong thing, so I didn't say or do anything. I feared him and how much worse this relationship could end up being. I no longer trusted or felt like I knew this person anymore.

One of his closest friends around this time was the nice lady who was probably twenty years older than us who had two young daughters. She had had a bit of a rough life herself and struggled financially, as did we. It seemed like Max and I were at her house quite often. Max would go to her when he was out of smokes and get them from her, which he said he would pay her back for, but of course, he never did. Some weeks, we were there every day; other weeks, it was twice a week. Occasionally, we slept over. I always felt bad because even though Max had no problem taking advantage of her hospitality, or of anybody really, I did. I didn't want to eat her food. She was broke, like us. I didn't feel it was right.

She and Max would always either go upstairs into her bedroom or go for a walk and smoke cigarettes or weed. I thought it was odd at first, but she explained to me that she didn't want her kids seeing them smoke weed. I joined them once or twice, but I never found it very interesting to talk about random, stupid stuff and smoke weed, so I usually stayed downstairs. I would either play outside or watch a movie with the kids. The girls weren't that young—they were ten and thirteen—so they must have known what their mother and Max were doing.

One day we were there and it was one of the girls' birthdays. As a gift, someone had gotten them BB guns. The girls were running around the house when we arrived, shooting at each other. There were screams whenever someone got hit. The girls told us that it was a set of four guns and the other two were on the table, so Max and I each grabbed one. I had never played with a BB gun, so I was quite excited. We all split up into teams. Max and I each had a kid on our team, and we all ran around the house shooting BBs at each other.

I was reluctant to hit Max, but he had no problem shooting me. It was fun, but he didn't like getting hit and after awhile he completely lost it. The girls were tired of the game by then, but Max was still hunting. He started targeting me and shooting me over and over. At first, I thought it was all in fun, but then I saw the look on his face. It was those black eyes again. I realized he wasn't playing anymore.

He kept coming after me. I told him I wouldn't shoot him anymore, but he said nothing and kept shooting me. I walked away and suddenly felt a sharp sting on my buttock. I turned around and gently rubbed where he had hit me. "Stop it, Max!" I said assertively. I turned around and began walking away when I felt the same sharp sting on the back of my head. All I could do was run away. I hid in one of the girls' bedrooms upstairs and leaned on the closed door. Max had followed me up the stairs, shot at the door for a while and then stopped.

I sat upstairs alone for thirty minutes or so. When it got quiet downstairs, I figured it was safe for me to come out. I left the gun in the room I had been hiding in and then opened the door, heading for the stairs. I turned the corner to go downstairs.

Max was standing halfway up the short staircase. On his way up, he froze and so did I. He had the gun in his hand and I was unarmed. "Max, I'm done playing. I don't have the gun anymore," I said to him, not sure what he was thinking. He took a couple of steps further up the stairs and towards me. I stepped back but I was up against a wall. I managed to let out a "Max, don't," but he had already raised the gun and aimed it at me.

"Max, please don't," I pleaded. I knew it would hurt, especially at such a close range. He aimed for the sensitive part of my upper thigh and didn't even hesitate. He pulled the trigger, shot me, and went back downstairs.

I was left writhing in pain. The sting from those tiny BBs was intense. I went into the bathroom and quickly undressed to access the injury that Max had inflicted upon me. My thigh had a huge red welt that had swelled up instantly and the back of my head was sore and stinging.

I had tiny red marks like chicken pox on my arms. I stood in front of the mirror and the longer I stood there, the more bruises I noticed. I looked like a morbid painter's canvas. My body had many shades of abuse. My new bruises were black and blue. The old ones were that weird yellow-green colour. I stood there, disturbed by my appearance.

I hurriedly and angrily dressed myself. I couldn't believe how someone could treat another person the way Max treated me. He told me he loved me, but this was not love. This was not the way you treated someone you love. I gave myself a stern look in the mirror before opening the door confidently and heading downstairs.

All three family members were now sitting together in the living room watching a movie. I headed straight for the coat rack. I grabbed my coat and started to put it on when Max quietly snuck up behind me and pushed me up against the wall. "Where do you think you're going?" he said, pushing his body up against mine so I was stuck between the wall and him. "Home," I said firmly.

"I don't think so," he said as he twisted me around so I was facing him. He put his hand on my throat. "Get off me," I said, pushing him away. His hand fell off my throat and made a fist.

I flinched and hesitated to speak, but I was able to manage some leverage. "Are you seriously thinking about hitting me right now? You are that comfortable with yourself being a woman beater that you're going to beat me up at your friend's house, when they are in the next room? Don't you dare lay one finger on me. You are an idiot."

I was so angry and utterly disgusted by the fact that he was now abusing me in other people's homes. He knew I was right. If he hit me and I yelled, everybody would know. And if they looked at me, they would see bruises. Then his friends would know our secret and that would be it. A small part of me wanted his friends to know; perhaps then the nightmare would be over.

He then wanted me to sit and pretend like nothing happened, like I wasn't in pain. "Come and sit down with us. We're starting a movie. And keep your mouth shut. No one wants to hear you complaining," he commanded.

I stood there with a determined gaze. I was not going to sit with him. I couldn't stand to be near him. He unclenched his hand and swiftly turned on his heel, heading back towards the living room where everyone sat, the family never suspecting what almost happened in their home.

I grabbed my purse and left the house. I couldn't believe that he had treated me like this for so long. I didn't know if he forgot where he was or what happened but he was comfortable hitting me anywhere now, not just at

CHAPTER 9

home. I was absolutely appalled. That was the last time I went to that house.

That night, he spent the night there—I assumed since he hadn't come home—which is what I preferred anyways. I didn't hear from Max for a few days after that. I heard from his friends that he was still there at his friend's house. He'd stay there until they ran out of weed or cigarettes, most likely.

A week later, Max came back home. Whenever he came home after being gone for a few days, he was in a better mood and he was nice to me for a day or two. We tiptoed around each other and were polite, but it didn't last too long. Soon, we'd be arguing about something else stupid.

One day, I was struggling to cook a nice meal and multitask while arguing with Max and all of a sudden, I smelt something like smoke, something burnt. I had totally forgotten about the meat in the oven. Max had distracted me with a silly argument. I opened the oven door and smoke billowed out. Max continued to argue as I went to open the front door and tried to usher the smoke out the window with the kitchen towel.

While I was preoccupied with getting rid of the smoke, Max was searching the kitchen. I suddenly became aware of his opening and closing drawers methodically. He was grumbling to himself, and I couldn't make out what he was saying except the occasional swear word.

I grew a little anxious as I wasn't exactly sure what he was doing. I quietly closed the door and headed back to the kitchen. "Can I help you find something?" I asked, trying not to irritate him. He slowly turned his head to where I was standing, the corners of his mouth turned upwards and a devilish grin appeared on his face. *Oh no, not again,* I thought. I felt the hairs on the back of my neck stand up.

From the knife drawer he was standing in front of, Max gently pulled out a long knife with big teeth, the one you would use to cut into a roast. He gripped the handle as he drew it up and admired it. He slowly walked towards me.

"Max, what are you doing? Put that down right now," I said shakily, backing up away from him. *Last time it was a smaller knife and he just threatened me with it. What is he going to do this time?*

CHAPTER 10

The Promise Ring

I was terrified as I slowly backed away from Max and towards the bedroom doorway. He slowly came towards me with a still tight grip on the knife, holding it up in front of him with the teeth of the blade pointed in my direction. His eyes bounced back and forth between me and the knife. I took a quick step, and I was in the bedroom. I closed the door and pushed my back up against it. I sensed him standing on the other side of the door. Time stood still as did we.

"Max, can you please put that thing away?" I said, trying to sound calm. My thoughts were racing and all I could think about was how to escape. The door to the bedroom had no lock and I knew that if he pushed on the door enough, I wouldn't be able to hold him back forever. He was much stronger than me and full of rage—an unpredictable, dangerous and evil fury.

He knocked on the door.

"Go away," I said in distress. I knew that as soon as he came into the room, all hell would break loose.

He turned the handle and pushed on the door. I braced my body and dug my heels into the carpet. He began pushing the door harder and harder, taking short breaks in between each push. I stayed put until I realized I wouldn't be able to hold the door much longer. My eyes frantically searched the room for a way out, or something to hide under and the distance each option was from the door. I had an open window and a sticky side door leading outside; it would get jammed often and it wouldn't always open.

He backed away from the door for a second. All was eerily quiet. Next thing I knew, I heard fast footsteps and realized he was hurtling at the door. I had seconds to make a move. When he was in monster mode, there was no going back.

I ran to the bed, jumping on it where the open window was. I set one foot on the window ledge as Max hurled

CHAPTER 10

himself at the door and it burst open with a crash, smashing the wall behind it. I looked out the window quickly. We were on the second floor and there was tall grass below. I was contemplating the jump and hoping not to get hurt as I would have to run if I jumped out. I'd have to run past the door where Max could catch me if he was faster than I was.

When I looked back up into the room, Max had recovered from almost falling as he was expecting the door to still be blocked by my body. He was standing ten feet away from me.

"Get out of my house!" I wailed with a shaky voice, "I don't want you here anymore. The police station is just up the road. I'll go there." He took a few steps closer and as he did, I got ready to jump out of the window if he didn't back off.

"No," he said quietly. "You don't want me anymore," he went on, his voice becoming gradually louder, "You're going to bring the cops, are you now?"

I didn't answer him. I didn't want to upset him more. I just wanted this nightmare to be over. I had one foot on the window ledge and the other out the window with my body hanging over the grass.

"Max, if you don't leave, I will jump out of this window," I warned him, also confirming to myself that I would have to do what was necessary to escape him. He simply shrugged his shoulders before throwing the knife in my direction, narrowly missing me and hitting the wall right next to the window that I was hanging halfway out of.

"Get out!" I shrieked, panicking.

He walked over to the sticky side door and fought with it to open. He took one last look at me before opening the door wide and walking out.

I propelled myself off the ledge, pouncing back into the room onto the bed and then onto the ground. I stumbled towards the open side door and slammed it shut. I leaned the chair up against the door with the headrest under the handle. Then, I had a thought and ran from the bedroom through the kitchen, then through the living room to the front door and locked it. I went back to the bedroom and closed and locked the window that just seconds ago I was about to jump out of.

I peeked through the curtain on the side door, searching for Max to see if he was hanging around or if he had, in fact, left. I couldn't see him, so I walked back to the front of the house and looked out the window to check if he was there anywhere. I caught a quick glimpse of his back walking up the road and heading towards his friend's house.

CHAPTER 10

I was shaking. I didn't want him back in my house. I went back to the kitchen and grabbed garbage bags from under the sink before heading to the bedroom. I put all his clothes into two large garbage bags. I waited for maybe an hour, sitting on my bed, trembling. I needed to make sure the coast was clear.

I finally peered through the curtain to look outside for Max and locate the empty garbage bin. The last thing I needed was for Max to catch me throwing his clothes out into the garbage; he would certainly beat me for that. When I felt sure that he was no longer around, I grabbed the two big bags and ran outside, threw them in the garbage bin and closed the lid before running back into my room, slamming the door behind me and locking it.

My heart was racing. I was terrified, mad, upset and yet I felt empowered. I knew this kind of life had to end. If he was now comfortable threatening my life with weapons, I knew things would only get worse from here. I sat there thinking of what my next move should be. I knew he would come back. He always did.

My brain and heart were confused and hurt. Did I still love this man who had caused me so much pain? I didn't know the answer to that question. A part of me still wanted to make it work, but another more sensible part of me knew that I didn't need someone like him in my life. I hoped that when he did come back, he would notice the garbage bags. They weren't completely hidden, so I figured he would get the point. Luckily, he didn't have keys to the doors. The front door was massive and made of solid cedar; you would need an axe for sure to break that door down. The side door to my bedroom, however, was not as solid or strong; it was old and could probably be broken without too much difficulty.

I didn't sleep much that night, if at all. All of my senses where heightened. I was awake, waiting and listening for any sound, a footstep or maybe a knock on the door, even the rustling of garbage bags or the garden gate squeaking open. I lay in my bed frozen with fear.

All night, I waited to hear sounds that, thankfully, I never heard. I had mustered the courage to tiptoe to the side door and very carefully make a small hole in the blinds to peak outside. With the streetlights, I could make out the garbage bags still in the cans and I could see the road. No sign of Max.

I had eventually fallen asleep and was awakened suddenly by something. The sun was now rising. I listened and looked around me, but I didn't hear a sound. I thought it must have been a dream, so I curled back into my bed

CHAPTER 10

when I heard a quiet knock on my bedroom door that led to the outside. Then I heard a voice gently call my name.

"Joy. Joy. Are you awake? It's me. It's Max," he said quietly, comfortingly. But I froze. He must have climbed up to the second story door knowing I had locked myself in the bedroom where everything had occurred.

I was quiet in hopes that he would give up and leave. "Please come and open the door. I'm deeply sorry about yesterday. Please let me talk with you." His voice was small and pathetic. "I'm sorry for my behaviour and how I treated you. I love you so much. I don't want to be without you."

Then his voice became sniffly like he was trying not to cry. "I love you and I need you. I know I'm fucked up. You're the only one who can love me. Please, Joy, let me in. I need you."

A tiny part of my heart went out to him, but I stayed put comfortably in my bed. I was determined. "Your belongings are outside in the garbage bins. There is nothing else for you here," I yelled as I was in bed across the room. I put the pillow over my head, but I could still hear him talking through the door. "I need to speak with you. Please give me a chance to apologize."

I slowly and reluctantly got up and peered out the window of the front of the house. Max was standing there on the porch outside the door, his head hanging low and looking quite sorry for himself. He was alone, and the garbage bags had been pulled out of the garbage bins but left there on the pathway. I took a deep breath and tried to compose myself. I was shaking but I didn't want him to see me scared and weak. I unlocked the door and opened it slightly. Max lifted his head and looked at me. Taking a step back, he said, "I'm so so sorry, Joy. Please forgive me." I didn't know what to say, so I didn't say anything, I crossed my arms. Before I knew it, he was kneeling down on one knee. My jaw hit the floor in disbelief as I couldn't believe what I was seeing. *Is he going to propose to me?*

He slowly brought his hand forward from behind his back and presented me with a huge bouquet of red roses. I gasped in utter shock. I gently accepted the flowers from his hands and thanked him. He knew I loved roses. I closed my eyes to smell them and they smelt beautiful. When I opened my eyes, Max was fumbling in his pocket. He brought out a small brown ring box. My astonishment must have shown as he quickly opened the box to show a rather large ring, with a large stone, my birthstone. I searched his face for any hint of what was to come. "This is not an engagement ring, don't worry," he said quickly before I could say anything. I was stunned as I didn't know what it was supposed to be if not an engagement ring.

CHAPTER 10

"It's a promise ring. A promise to no longer hurt you. I will not lay another finger on you. I couldn't stand to lose you. I would die without you and I don't want you with anyone else," he said, standing up and reaching for my hand. I began to cry. He was so sincere in that moment, even he had tears in his eyes, though they did not fall.

He reached for me and pulled me close to his body. He held me tight yet so gently, lovingly, tenderly. This was the Max that I loved. We stood there on the small porch holding each other and crying for some time. I don't know what was going through his mind but mine was moving at lightning speed thinking about what I was going to do. It was clear that we still cared very deeply for each other, so I didn't want things between us to end. After a few more moments, I wiped the tears from my face and broke the silence. "I should put these in some water quickly," I said, brushing away more tears and looking at the beautiful bouquet of roses.

I dropped my arms from around him and turned, heading back into the house and towards the kitchen in search of a vase. He melted my heart with the romantic gestures and I let him in once again. He was being the old romantic Max that I was in love with. He followed me into the room and throughout the house to the kitchen where he leaned against the cabinet as I laid the bouquet on the table and searched for scissors.

I enjoyed unwrapping the flowers and organizing them tenderly into a vase. I moved in slow motion as I pulled out each rose, separating it from the rest, admiring it before cutting the bottom of the stem and then placing it into the vase. We admired the bouquet in its proper vase and I placed it on my dresser where I could easily view it. We stood there looking at the roses and our reflection in the mirror behind them. I felt and watched through the mirror as Max lifted both his hands slowly and put them around me. He hugged me gently as he tenderly placed a kiss on the back of my head.

He then headed to the bathroom. When I was alone, it was then that I had the courage to look at this new ring on my finger. I was still puzzled as to what it was supposed to represent. I wasn't sure why he bought me a ring. He must have been searching for anything that would make me forgive him for his cruel and painful treatment. He had made it clear that it was not an engagement ring. He said it was a promise to no longer hurt me. But in those terrifying moments, I doubted a ring would prevent him from raising a fist at me. How could I know that I was safe and trust him to not hurt me again?

CHAPTER 10

It was very confusing to me. There was a point in our relationship where I would have been more than thrilled to be given a ring by Max, but this didn't feel right. It didn't feel the way I thought it should. I wasn't overcome with love or excitement.

Looking at the ring, I noted the thick silver band, quite thick, very much like a man's ring. If I were to pick a ring out myself, I would not have chosen this one. It was not my taste. At least he had gotten the correct birthstone—but it was held by a gold circle. It was big and took up the front of my entire finger. The ring itself was also much too big. It only fit my thumb.

After being together for three years, you would think that he would know what kind of ring I would like. But it's a ring of apology. I can't be choosy, so I'll accept it as that. An apology ring. I told myself it was the gesture that counted, that it showed that he did care and that he was committed to me. Max walked in, tearing me from my thoughts. "Do you like the ring?"

I didn't want to lie to him, but I also didn't want to hurt his feelings. I smiled and nodded before replying yes. I had taken the ring off to admire it as it didn't look good on my hand. It was back in the ring box on the dresser with the lid open when Max walked in and asked me what I thought.

I felt bad for lying, but he had made this grand gesture. I wanted to show appreciation for it.

I hoped I would grow to like it, but I never did. I asked him how he knew what my birthstone was. "You showed it to me once," he replied. I didn't remember this event, but I figured he wouldn't lie about it, so I accepted it as an answer.

He kissed me ever so tenderly on my forehead, then my cheeks, lingering his lips on each cheek for a moment. He pulled his head away and looked deep into my eyes with an apologetic look, a look that was asking me to let him back into my heart. I gave a small smile.

"I love you, Joy," he whispered. I simply nodded.

He leaned in and paused for a second before kissing me on the lips. Then, he kissed me again.

No matter what happened, we always seemed to have a good sexual connection. That is the way we came back to each other, the way we would find each other again. He kissed me until I kissed him back. He then moved down and started kissing my neck. He knew that was my secret spot.

He took his sweater off and kissed me with deep, hot passion, holding me tightly in his arms. He then proceeded to undress slowly while kissing me. I felt his hand reaching for the bottom of my shirt to pull it up over my head. I hesitated for a second, and then I let him remove my shirt.

He began to kiss my body while removing each article of clothing slowly and sensually. My body was covered in goosebumps. I wasn't sure if I should give into him or not. I was nervous, as if it was the first time all over again.

I wasn't in the mood, but I really needed to be reassured that he loved me. Being passionate with someone can validate your feelings for them and theirs for you. I needed and craved that validation as if my life depended on it.

I gave into him and we made passionate love. Afterwards, we lay there, his arms cradled around me. We lay there in silence with our hearts open to each other, simply enjoying the powerful passion we had just shared. I fell asleep with the warmth of his body on mine. I slept peacefully for the first time in a long time.

For about a week after he gave me the flowers and ring, I would wake up in the morning and the first thing I would see was the beautiful red roses. I couldn't help but smile at their beauty. Then, my eyes would move to the ring box that was now closed. I didn't need the box to be open to know what the ring looked like. I had worn it a couple of times around Max, but it really wasn't a pretty ring.

Things between Max and I were much better again and we got along. His habits of wandering off and spending the day away from me never changed, but he came back every night. Some nights we would make love, some nights it was fun sex. But even though we had come back to each other, it still felt like there was a big rift between us. Something that could not be ignored and something that would not go away, no matter how many nights we shared together. I waited for this feeling to go away. I waited for the gap between us to eventually shrink, but it was always there, lurking in the back of my mind like a ghost.

After the incident with the knife, I wanted to make sure it would never happen again. One day when Max was out, I hurriedly went through all the cupboards searching for knives. I left only the knives to eat with—basically just the butterknives. I left a few paring knives in one drawer so it didn't look suspicious as if I were hiding them.

I wrapped all the knives in a shirt to put under my father's bed. My father's room was at the other end of the house. Max had no reason to ever go into my father's room, so I had begun hiding valuables in there. Once the knives were hidden, I felt safer, but if Max suspected anything at all, it would only cause trouble. My fate rested on him not noticing anything was different.

CHAPTER 11

The Party

Weeks went by and life continued. Eventually, the arguing began again, and Max's tantrums and the abuse. I hadn't been out in public for a while. I was lonely and depressed. New Year's was approaching, so I decided to reach out to a few friends and have a small party.

When I called my friends to give them the date, time and address of my New Year's Eve celebration, most were shocked but delighted to hear from me. I had been missing in action for quite some time, so they were eager to hang out.

Max's idea of a party was sitting on a smelly couch with smoke filling the air and drinking beer with his friends and getting high. That was not my idea of fun, nor was it a hopeful way to ring in the new year either.

I informed Max that I was planning a get-together for my friends and I to catch up as I hadn't seen them in ages. I told him there was to be only a handful of people—that was what I wanted. An intimate gathering was what I had in mind. I asked him to refrain from inviting his friends as they were vastly different from mine, and I didn't think they would be a good fit. I told him he was welcome to join us—but no friends. I didn't want anyone at my party to feel uncomfortable or awkward, so I pressed the fact that he could not invite friends over.

He was, of course, upset and told me he had made plans with his own friends, so he would be gone anyway. I was relieved to hear this, at the thought of no drama for a night. My friends didn't approve of Max; they simply tolerated him for my sake.

My friends were like I was before I had met Max. They were kind and thoughtful. They didn't party. They didn't smoke weed or cigarettes. And most importantly, I could trust them.

Max's friends, on the other hand, partied a lot and got stupid drunk. They would likely hotbox the house and I'd never get the smell out. It wasn't fun to party with them as I always ended up babysitting, which meant I could never

CHAPTER 11

enjoy myself. I had had my fill of his friends for the last two and a half years. I wanted my friends back. I started to want more than just Max. I wanted other people around me.

I was ecstatic to be planning something for myself. The day before the party I spent cleaning the entire house from top to bottom. I wanted the house to be perfect so it looked like a normal house—not a warzone. I was sure to clean up any signs of the hidden life I was living. I had also blocked off areas where I didn't want people going just in case. I put a bookcase in front of my dad's bedroom door and I closed mine. I also had a huge set of shelves put in front of the basement door as my dad had lots of stuff down there. Anything that was valuable or breakable that I hadn't previously hidden from Max was put on my father's bed. I wanted to cover all my bases just in case the party got out of control. I wanted to be prepared.

The day of the party came and people started to arrive around 9 p.m. I greeted my guests at the door. Many asked if Max was around and I informed them he was out for the night and wouldn't be joining us. They somehow knew that meant we could freely talk and be ourselves.

We began pouring drinks, chatting and laughing. It was a little awkward at first as they talked about things I had not known about, so I felt a little left out. Their lives had kept moving forward while mine seemed stagnant. I hadn't expected the awkwardness, so it threw me off even more than missing out on fun adventures.

I could tell my friends felt the awkward cloud over our heads. They quickly changed the subject so I could share in the conversation. They asked me what I had been up to as well as how living on our own was. Of course, I couldn't share everything with them, so I tried to only share the good stuff. I told them stories of work and that I had lost my job, so I was spending my days trying to find another one. I made it a quick, short story, not detailed as to the reasoning for me losing my job. The idea of living on my own was still a glamourous idea to them as they all lived with their parents still. They had not experienced the hardships of working to survive.

The living room was peaceful—nothing but joyful chatter and music playing quietly in the background. After we were all caught up, it felt like no time had passed since last I saw them. It was so nice to be with my friends again. No drama, no stress.

Suddenly, there was a knock at the door. I hoped it wasn't Max arriving to either ruin the party or end it. He was supposed to be out with friends, so I could only imagine the state he'd be in.

CHAPTER 11

I was relieved to open the door and see my friend Kate. She had brought a date with her. Kate had gone to school with most of us, so she knew most of the people that night. She apologized for her lateness and introduced her date to everyone. His name was James. He fit in well with the crowd and soon it was like he was one of us. We were chatting away, playing a few drinking games. It was the most fun I'd had in ages. I was able to be my old fun-loving self. I hadn't been able to be myself without stressing for a very long time.

James didn't bring any alcohol with him, so he wanted to go grab some. My best friend Jon wanted more alcohol, so the three of us headed out on foot up the road to the small liquor store on the corner. It was a quick trip and no one back at the house was drunk, so I wasn't worried.

When we arrived back at the house thirty minutes later, there was an uncomfortable shift in the atmosphere. It was very odd. My friends who had been hanging out in the living room had all gone into my bedroom. I wondered why they had moved from the living room as the three of us walked in to join them. I heard a few different voices coming from the room that I could not identify.

When I entered the room, there was Max, already drunk, in the room and he had brought along two friends: Brad, who he had been friends with for years, and Alisha, Brad's newest girlfriend who I had seen once or twice before.

Max stumbled towards me and planted a wet, drunken kiss on me. He smelled like a brewery. I pulled him aside and demanded to know why he had brought his friends when I asked him not to. "We were bored, so we thought we'd check out your party. Don't worry we will behave ourselves," he pretended to reassure me.

"I don't want anyone smoking in the house," I asserted, "And please keep an eye on your friends. I don't want any trouble."

Max and his friends would fight and be stupid when drinking. The three of them were drunk and stoned and I suspected that they had also done cocaine. I decided I would let it go. I didn't want to ruin the party or be the one to make it weird, so I went and said hello to Brad and Alisha to not seem rude. I introduced my friends to them and my friends were very respectful, but it was very obvious that my friends and Max's friends were from completely different worlds.

As the night went on, more and more of Max's friends began to pop up at the house. I was so upset; this was supposed to be my night with my friends and Max had gone and turned it into a huge party. My few friends were sitting

CHAPTER 11

in one part of the house talking amongst themselves and Max and his rowdy friends were in another room. About twelve people were spread about the house.

After an hour or so, it was obvious that everyone was wasted, but somehow there was still plenty of alcohol. Walking through the kitchen, I realized the shelf in front of the basement door had been moved, the door ajar. I peered in to see Brad and Max on the basement stairs.

"You aren't allowed down there," I said, distressed that Max had betrayed my trust. "Plus, there's rats down there," I added, hoping it would deter them. As soon as they came up, I slid the shelf back in front of the door, even moving the fridge out of the kitchen a bit and in front of the door to make it more difficult to get to.

Heading back to my friends, I noticed there was now a topless contest going on among the boys in Max's entourage. One particular friend of Max's, Tom, was beyond drunk and had removed all his clothing except his boxers. Tom was a nice enough guy who frequently partied with Max and only lived a few blocks away from my dad's house. When he had heard about my party, he invited himself.

One moment he was running through the house and the next, he seemed to have disappeared. I hoped he had gone home as he didn't live very far.

Thirty minutes later, there was a loud knock at the door. I instantly shot Max a look that inquired if he was expecting anyone else. He just shrugged. I walked over to the front door hoping that it wasn't yet another uninvited friend of Max's. I reluctantly opened the door.

I was a bit drunk at this point, so I couldn't help but laugh a little when standing at my front door was my unimpressed elderly neighbour holding Tom by the ear as if she were his mother. Tom was buck naked with a huge grin on his face. I tried to look horrified, but it was quite a funny sight to see.

"Does this belong to you?" the old lady asked as she looked me up and down with an angry face.

She asked when my father would return and said she would be telling him about this incident. I apologized profusely and pleaded for her not to tell my father as he would be upset to know I had thrown a party. She shoved him at me and abruptly left. Before closing the garden gate behind her, she told me to keep it down.

"Well, hello there, pretty lady," he said to me before slipping past me to join the party. Tom was welcomed back into the house by Max's friends like a champion as the other topless guys pounded their chests like gorillas.

Max's friend, Brad, began bugging his girlfriend to remove her shirt and "join the fun," as he put it. She had particularly large breasts and he wanted her to show them off. She hesitated and looked at me. "I'll take mine off if you take yours off," she offered. I crossed my arms across my chest. *I'm not taking mine off.*

Alisha reluctantly obliged, distracted by Brad who was making out with her and helping her remove her shirt. I was sitting on the desk with my arms and legs crossed. A couple of the boys, including Max, branded me as being no fun, telling me to remove my shirt and let loose. I flat out refused. The idea of being half naked in front of these drunken buffoons was not appealing in the slightest. I would not give into the peer pressure as Alisha had.

The boys then became rougher and more determined to get my shirt off. A few of them tried to grab my shirt and pull it off. I slapped at their hands and repeatedly said no. "C'mon, we're just having fun!" They continued to chant for me to remove my shirt. Even Alisha tried to convince me. "It's not that bad. Just take it off and they'll leave you alone." She tried to sound calm and persuasive. I didn't budge.

I could sense some people leaving the room. The atmosphere had changed again, this time more animalistic. The room was now filled with Max's people and mine had migrated to another part of the house. It was now extremely uncomfortable.

"No, leave me alone!" I repeatedly told them. Then, Max came barging through. "Have some fun, Joy. You never let loose. Take it off. It's no big deal. Nothing we haven't all seen before." He laughed. "Stop being such a prude. Take your shirt off," he scolded.

He told me I was being a party pooper and ruining everyone's buzz. Again, I refused, so he reached for my shirt to pull it off me and I was stuck. I was sitting on a desk against the wall and in front of me was Tom, Brad and Max telling me to remove my shirt. It all happened so quickly. Hands were all over me and the shirt I was wearing was literally torn off my body. I stood there topless, thankfully with my bra still on, but completely violated. I was furious. Warm tears built up in my eyes.

As soon as my shirt was off, the boys stepped back. I tried to cover myself with my arms and pieces of my shirt. I jumped off the desk and headed for the other room. Max scooped me up in his arms and took me to the bed, which was in the corner of the room. He was drunk and aroused. He started kissing me all over and grabbing at my breasts. I was panicked at the thought of him forcing himself on me in front of all these people. This was a side of Max I had not seen.

I tried pushing him off me. He was determined and held my arms tightly as he whispered what he wanted to do in my ear. At first, I tried to reason with him. I told him that after everyone left we could have sex. I told him I wasn't comfortable and that I didn't want to have sex in front of other people. He wouldn't stop, so I struggled to wiggle my body out from under him. "Max, get off me! I mean it. Stop this!" I said it louder this time, "We are NOT having sex right now!" I pushed him.

He continued slurring his wet words into my ears and touching me. He smelt so bad. I was repulsed by his behaviour and wanted nothing to do with him. "C'mon baby. No one's watching. Let's do it," he insisted. I became frantic at the thought of not being able to stop him. Behind us, the guys continued to talk amongst themselves, but no one left or helped. After what felt like a long time, I was finally able to roll him off me and off the bed.

I got up quickly and ran to the other room where I knew my friend Jon was. Jon looked up at me, quickly took his shirt off and draped it over me. He had on an undershirt, which made me feel more comfortable as I had been staring at unwelcome naked bodies all night.

He asked me if I was okay and I said I was fine, but I wasn't. I was so angry. I felt powerless as I sat in the room with my friends while the rowdy bunch stayed in the other room. Jon had been playing chess with James and he had his arm around me. I sat next to him feeling so small. I apologized to my friends for Max's behaviour, blaming everyone's lewdness on the liquor. More excuses on my part. In that moment, I sincerely questioned why I always defended Max.

After about an hour, we heard yelling and swearing from the rowdy bunch. Some guys were arguing. Jon and I went to investigate. Tom and Max had been fighting when Tom pulled out a knife. The other boys attempted to placate Tom as Max threatened him further. Then, Max pulled out his own blade.

CHAPTER 12

My Final Breath

"Stop! Put the knives down," I yelled, "You guys can go outside if you want, but this is not happening in my house!"

I glared at Tom. "You can leave," I said to him.

They put their knives away. Tom apologized to me and left. "This party is over," I said, this time deflated. It was more than I had bargained for when I came up with the idea to throw a New Year's Eve party. I was so drained by the events of the evening, I wanted to crawl up in a corner and stay there. I was still shaken by Max's behaviour with me.

After letting Max's posse out, I went back to the bedroom. Max was passed out on the floor. He had grabbed the comforter from the bed and was curled up in it. I was happy he was asleep; it meant there wouldn't be any more stupid shit happening in my house. I was also relieved that I would not have to lie next to him in bed after how he had humiliated me.

A couple of my friends had stayed behind as they wanted to make sure I—and the house—were okay. We sprawled out on the couches and reflected on the chaos of the evening. After a few moments, James stumbled to his feet and told us he was going home.

I asked him if he wanted me to call him a cab, but he said he had his car and was fine driving home. I disagreed. I asked him where his car keys were. He pulled them out from the pocket of his jeans, waving them in front of my face. I looked at him disappointed and quickly grabbed the keys from his hands. "James, you are way too drunk to drive. You can sleep in the spare room and leave in the morning," I asserted as I put his keys in my pocket.

At first, he didn't want to stay, but the others talked him into it. He was new to drinking as he had just turned nineteen and didn't know his limits yet. It took a few of us to walk him over to the guest room and he fell face-first onto the bed. He was so tall his legs hung off. A couple of us tried to move him in a more comfortable position, but he was so big, we couldn't accomplish such a feat.

As we turned to leave the guest room, we heard a gagging, rough coughing sound. James had turned over and thrown up all over the side of the bed and floor. I went to the laundry room and grabbed a dirty towel. We cleaned him up and the side of the bed as best we could for the time being. "Oh my god. I am so sorry," he apologized with shame. "Its okay," I reassured him, "Everyone throws up at least once in their life from drinking too much. Don't worry about it. But you are definitely cut off."

I handed him one of Max's shirts that he never wore. I went to the kitchen to get a bucket and a glass of water. I laid the bucket and the water beside him on the bedside table and told him they were there. He was barely conscious sprawled out on the bed, so I didn't know if he heard me or not. I put a blanket over him. He began snoring before we even closed the bedroom door. After James was soundly asleep, we called cabs for the remainder of the party guests.

After everyone had left, I looked around the house and took in the aftermath of the party. The house was a complete mess. Liquor bottles and cans everywhere. The furniture had been moved all around. The chess board was still out and there was puke nearby. The bookcase in front of my dad's bedroom door had been moved, again, and a few people seemed to have been in there. I quickly glanced inside. Everything appeared to be as I had left it. I wanted to clean up, but it was four in the morning. I was drunk and exhausted from the madness. I decided I would do it when I woke up.

I learnt a particularly good lesson that night: *Never throw a party at your own house.* I headed to my bedroom and noticed that Max had gotten up and onto the bed, now splayed out in a drunken slumber, taking up the whole bed. I pushed him over with some difficulty so I would have room to fit myself. I pulled the covers over my body and quickly fell asleep.

I woke up with a massive migraine. Memories from the night before came flooding back in. I thought of the mess that awaited me, and then I remembered that there was still a party guest in the guest room.

I went to see if James was awake, but he was still passed out, snoring loudly. I had forgotten he had thrown up until I noticed the amount of vomit we had missed on the floor and down the side of the bed. I cringed at the thought of having to clean it up. I decided I would shower and once

CHAPTER 12

I was done and dressed, I would wake him up if he wasn't already awake. I went to the bedroom to grab my towel.

I smelt of liquor and cigarettes. My chest felt sticky, like someone had spilled their drink on me, although I didn't remember any such incident. I locked the bathroom door and looked in the mirror. I looked tired and pale, ugly. I quickly undressed and threw my clothes in the laundry hamper. I had slept in my sticky, stinky clothes.

I turned the water on and waited for it to become hot. I stepped into the bath and let the hot water run down my body. It was ecstasy. I could feel all the slime and disgusting feelings from the night before just wash away. The steam began to build up in the bathroom. I loved my hot showers. I wished I could stay in the hot stream of water all day and not have to clean the house. I was daydreaming, relishing the nice, quiet moment until I realized I should probably hurry up and wash my hair so I could get out and get to work. I knew cleaning the house was going to be another all-day thing.

I scrubbed the syrupy liquor off my body. As I washed my hair, flashes of what had happened barged into my focus. I thought of Tom running around naked, the guys' horrible behaviour, my shirt being torn from my body, the way Max had treated me. He hadn't stuck up for me when they wanted me to remove my shirt; he encouraged it and tried to force himself on me in front of everyone. I was so embarrassed. I was also furious. The more I thought about it, the more I became angry with Max and his overall behaviour. I quickly rinsed my hair and jumped out of the shower. I didn't want to think about Max anymore; it just made me mad.

I had to concentrate on getting the house back in order. I dried myself, wrapped myself in a towel and headed towards the bedroom. I hurriedly grabbed a clean shirt and some shorts. Max was still passed out in bed. As I got dressed, I was slowly starting to feel better. Standing in front of the mirror, I tied my hair up in a bun and out of my face. Having had a shower, I was now ready to tackle my day. I quickly turned and headed out of the room.

I went back to the guest room to see if James was awake. I gently knocked on the door and peered around the corner to see James lying on his back, yawning and stretching his arms wide. His head fell to the side, and he blinked when he noticed me. I gave him a small nod while holding one of Max's shirts out to him. He sat up and slowly grabbed the shirt. He slipped out of the shirt he had vomited on and slept in before putting on the clean shirt. I handed him the glass of water that I had left for him the night before. He thanked me and gulped the water down.

CHAPTER 12

"How do you feel?" I asked, handing him some aspirin. I could tell he was still drunk. "I feel really shitty. I'm sorry again about the puke," he said sheepishly.

"Well, I need to clean up the place. It's a total mess. But I don't think you're fit to drive home, so I can call a friend or parent to come pick you up. You can come back later or tomorrow to pick up your car," I told him, smiling.

"Yeah, that's probably a good idea. My head is pounding. I don't think I can drive," he said before pulling out his phone to call someone. While we waited, we chatted a bit as I did not know much about him. I told him he could shower if he wanted, but he preferred to wait until he got home. I insisted he at least brush his teeth and he agreed; his breath was rancid. It wasn't long until his friend showed up. We had been waiting for him on the porch. His friend and I had to help James down the stairs. Even though we each grabbed a side, he was crooked and almost fell a few times on the way to the car.

I didn't want to leave any evidence of the party I had thrown. My father would be livid. The house that I had thoroughly cleaned only twenty-four hours prior was now a disaster. I went to the kitchen and grabbed several garbage bags. I collected all the empty liquor bottles and put them in one trash bag; in another, I put all the leftover food and garbage that was laying around.

I noticed objects that had been moved from their places, such as ornaments and pictures hanging slightly crooked on the wall. I adjusted them as I went along. I heard the bedroom door open and Max came out. His eyes were barely open, and he dragged his feet as he headed towards the bathroom. "Good morning," I said as he closed the door behind him. He looked horrible and probably felt about as good as he looked. I smirked as I thought to myself that he deserved it.

After I finished with the dishes in the sink, I headed to the guest room to confront the vomit. I put my hand over my nose and mouth. The smell was sharp. As I looked about the room, I wondered how to best clean it all up. I had never had to clean up something of this substance. I headed back towards the kitchen and searched in the cleaning closet for whatever I could use. I grabbed a bunch of chemicals, not even knowing if they mixed well or not, as well as a mop and bucket. I went to the kitchen sink and began to fill the bucket with scalding hot water, Pine-Sol and bleach. Max came through the kitchen just then as I was making my concoction and glanced at me.

"I would really appreciate some help as your friends helped to make the mess," I said to him sternly. This caused

CHAPTER 12

him to take his eyes off me and go back to the bedroom. He closed the door behind him and I was left alone again. Taking care of everything on my own as I always did.

I picked up the bucket and the mop and walked back to the guest room. I put the bucket down by the entrance of the door and contemplated my next move. *Should I wash the entire floor or just the spot with the vomit? Should I sweep first? Should I try a paper towel?* The thought of picking up vomit in a paper towel made me dunk the mop in the hot soapy water instead. I washed the spot methodically, moving the mop back and forth, then wringing it out in the bucket before dunking the mop and doing it all over again.

Once I felt the floor was clean, I set the mop down next to the bucket. I stripped the bed and tidied the room. I brought the sheets to the laundry room and put them in the washer, adding bleach before turning it on. As I came through the living room, I noticed Max sitting quietly at the computer on Facebook, head down, typing away. It had already been a couple of hours since I began cleaning and I was exhausted.

I put down the bucket of dirty water I was about to dump in the toilet and walked towards Max. "I would *really* appreciate some help, Max. I've already done most of it, but I would appreciate help with the rest." I stared at his back waiting for a response. He ignored me, so I stepped closer to see what was so important.

Past his shoulder, I saw he was having a conversation with a girl. I guiltily read a little of the conversation before realizing what I was reading. This was a very private, intimate conversation between two people who had made plans to see each other and have sex.

I couldn't believe it. Before thinking, I blurted, "What the fuck is this? What's going on? Who is this girl?" I was so upset at the thought that after everything we had been through, Max was possibly cheating on me. I stared at him in disbelief as he coldly responded with "It's none of your fucking business," never once taking his eyes off the computer. I was appalled at his nonchalant reaction to this. I took a step closer to him. I could feel anger swelling up in me.

"Max," I said louder. I wanted answers. "What is this? Who is she?" I waited again for some semblance of acknowledgement, but he remained enraptured in his online activities. He continued to type. I read further up in the conversation. Apparently, he told her we had broken up.

"This is my house and my computer, and you are not allowed to use it to cheat on me. You better explain yourself!" I could feel tears coming to the surface. He finally

CHAPTER 12

turned, but only to give me the death stare. He abruptly stood up and pushed past me. When he left the room, he had left his conversation open, so I decided to read it.

I sat down and scrolled to the beginning of the conversation. From what I could tell, they had worked together in the past and had been flirting for some time. The conversations were personal and intimate. He had made a few references about me as his ex-girlfriend. They had been in the middle of discussing what they wanted to do sexually with each other next time they were together. Even though I was reading the proof, I still couldn't believe that Max had been disloyal to me. I was so hurt; I felt my heart being ripped in half. This charade had been going on for a couple of weeks, if not longer, and I was completely oblivious to it.

I needed to figure out what was going on. I turned my chair in his direction. "Have you already had sex with her?" I asked him with anger and hurt in my voice. "I saw that you referred to me as your ex. Is that what you want?" I saw the anger in his eyes building. It was quick and sudden. His jaw was set in a straight line, his eyes shining with anger, and he spat crudely at me.

"I told you it wasn't any of your business. I can do what I want," he shouted and stormed across the room towards me. Faster than lightning, he grabbed my hair and began pulling me up off the chair and away from the computer. I screamed and grabbed his hand in my hair, attempting to pry his fingers apart to release me. He gripped tighter and when I struggled, he punched me in the gut. It happened so fast. I was not prepared. I felt the harsh blow and my knees gave in. There was another sharp pull of my hair as I fell to the ground. His one hand still held the top of my head as it throbbed. My gut hurt as I hit the floor, wishing this wasn't happening again.

"Why do you cause so much trouble? You make me so angry. Just leave me alone. I'm allowed to sleep with whoever I want. This isn't any of your business," Max shouted angrily at me before going on a rampage. Max barked at me, telling me how worthless I was and how it was my fault that he treated me this way. I thought about yelling back at him, telling him I wasn't worthless and how after he'd treated me so horribly, I'd still been honest and loyal to him. I didn't deserve to be treated this way—nobody did. But yelling back and arguing never led anywhere safe.

I sat up for fear he would kick me while I was crumpled on the floor. As soon as I got my head off the ground, I felt something hit my head. He was throwing anything he could find at me and the walls. Books, pictures, ornaments went flying in every direction. I yelled at him to stop, He

CHAPTER 12

was trashing my father's house and there wasn't anything I could do about it.

"Stop!" I screamed frantically, "Stop throwing things!" He began kicking me as I feared he would. He kicked my knees as I lay on the ground in the fetal position. I uncurled my legs, moving them away from his blows. His foot missed my knees but caught my stomach. He was yelling at me, filled with rage as he continued to throw things and kick me. I had heard it all before. He blamed me for his behaviour. Telling me that if I wasn't so nosy, if I just did what he told me to do, he wouldn't lose his temper. It was my fault yet again that he had resorted to physical acts of violence.

I lay there helpless as I watched the beautiful living room French glass door break completely. The pieces of glass that were still intact from the last time Max had slammed the door were now also broken glass shards, falling heavily to the ground as Max slammed the door once again. Just for the sake of it, he wanted to be as destructive as possible. As he was momentarily distracted, I thought I should get up as I was not safe on the ground. I watched him and tried to catch a moment when he wasn't looking at me to get up. The second he looked away, I lifted my head and began to move my arm under me to push myself up. I placed the palm of my hand firmly on the ground and then felt his hand on my throat as he leaned over my body. It happened in a flash. As soon as I had tried to push myself up, I was slammed back down, my head hitting the cold hardwood floor.

"God. I could kill you," he mumbled as he knelt over me. "You want me to help you clean up?" he mocked me louder and bolder. "I'll help you clean up, sure. I can help you." He paused for a second with his hand still held tightly around my neck.

My heart pounded in my chest and the blood pumped audibly in my neck. He gave me a strange look, as if trying to read my mind before he quickly released his hand from me and stood up. He turned his back to me and walked a few feet away before suddenly facing me again. He gave me a small sideways grin and then bent down to pick up the mop bucket of Pine-sol, vomit and bleach I hadn't yet disposed of. "Here's your help," he scowled, picking up the bucket of filth and covering me with it.

The water was ice cold and putrid. Looking around me, I noticed the broken glass and figurines that had been lovingly placed on the fireplace mantle now scattered all over the floor. I was covered in this disgusting sludge, feeling it seep through my clothes, soaking me and covering my hair.

CHAPTER 12

I sat in a puddle of misery as the water spread out onto the hardwood floor of the living room.

I looked up at Max in utter shock. He crouched down with one knee coming down hard onto my ribcage, pushing my ribs painfully into my lungs and making it hard to breathe. He knew that doing this would cause severe pain as I had had a horseback riding incident and had fractured a few ribs on each side. His weight on top of my fractured ribs felt like he might puncture a lung. I couldn't get a full breath. I started to panic.

I tried desperately to wiggle out from under his knee, but with every movement, the weight on my ribs felt heavier and sharper. He used his hands firmly to pin me down, holding my arms to the floor. The pain eventually became too much. I had to stop struggling; it only made it worse. I was having a hard-enough time breathing. He quickly adjusted himself, hovering above me and grabbing my throat with one hand and holding my other hand now positioned on my chest. My free hand immediately tried to pry his hand off my throat, but each attempt to tear his hand away seemed to fuel him into a stronger, tighter hold.

"Look what you make me do. Why do you make me so angry that I have to treat you like this? I hate you so much," he screamed, his eyes black and dead. He was the monster from hell in full form.

"Max," I tried to scream but I could only croak out a few sounds, "Max, Stop. Please! Stop, Max." I was pleading with the demon in his eyes to let me go, but he wouldn't. It had consumed him, and he no longer had control. I knew right then and there that I was going to die. He was too strong, and my struggling seemed to tighten his hand on my throat. My mind raced with thoughts of how I had let it get this far.

I struggled to pick my head up off the ground and it came up only an inch before Max slammed it back down onto the hard, cold, wet floor. My whole body hurt. I couldn't do anything at all. I had no more fight in me. I was seriously considering the thought of dying right there. My poor father would eventually come back from France to find his daughter dead on his living room floor. My breathing was getting slower. I couldn't swallow. He was squeezing my throat tighter. I felt like at any second my ribs would collapse and the weight of him would cause them to puncture my lungs.

I looked up at him, begging for him to stop with nothing but my eyes to communicate, tears pouring down my face. He looked back with apathy, no emotion except may-

CHAPTER 12

be a sense of satisfaction, knowing he was going to kill me this time. This was no longer the man that I had loved and fought for so fiercely. I did not love this man who lay on top of me, inflicting such horrible pain. After everything he had put me through, all the times I had let it slide, all the times I forgave him, this was how he thanked me.

My thoughts immediately went to the gratification he would get when I was finally dead. He would be rid of me and forget about me until he found another poor young woman to victimize. I did not want to let him have that. I didn't want him to have the power to decide when and if my life would end. If I was meant to die that day, I would have rather died some other way than by his doing, his own bare hands. I would have rather killed myself.

My head was already feeling fuzzy. I could feel myself floating in and out of consciousness due to the lack of oxygen. I felt extremely tired. I thought of how wonderful it would be to simply close my eyes and die. I decided right then and there that I would die in my own way and that I would be the one to kill myself.

I stopped crying and relaxed my body. I began to focus on what needed to be done. I had been quite an avid swimmer as a child, so I knew I could hold my breath for a while and thus slow my heart rate. My plan was to hold my breath for as long as possible, and when I couldn't hold it anymore, I would let out all the air and with the weight of his knee still on my ribs, I wouldn't be able to breathe anymore and I would slowly drift off and finally perish. I was ready.

I took as big of a breath as I could possibly muster and held it. When I was ready, I slowly let it out and then didn't inhale. I looked up at him over my body with his hand still around my throat and knee still on my ribs. I was angry inside but calm as I felt that I had taken my power back. I removed my hand from around the hand that was around my throat; I relaxed it at my side and closed my eyes.

Seconds rushed by as I held my breath. I could hear my heart beating loudly. It was a steady rhythmic sound that reverberated off the hardwood floor and rang loudly in my ears, steadily slowing down after every couple of beats. My lungs began to tighten, begging me to take a breath, but I wouldn't. *Not long now*, I thought.

I don't know how long I held my breath for. It felt like I had been lying there listening to my heartbeat and fighting the urge to breathe for a while. My consciousness drifted in and out. Everything became hazy and I passed out.

All of a sudden, I heard Max's voice, but I couldn't make out what he was saying. He was shaking me, his

CHAPTER 12

hands now off my throat and shaking my shoulders and touching my face. For a second, I had forgotten what had happened and where I was. His words became clear to me as he was pleading with me to breathe. His eyes were filled with remorse. His weight and knees were now off my ribs. I could breathe easier, but my body was still in shock and motionless.

His tears poured over my face as he leaned over me. He wrapped me up in his arms, cradling me like a child. I was dizzy and my throat felt sore with each breath I took. I lay in his arms limp like a doll, exhausted as never before. "I'm so sorry, Joy. Please, please forgive me. I promise I'll stop. I'll never lay another hand on you ever again. Please, just breathe. Breathe."

Am I dead or dreaming?

My body and head went numb.

CHAPTER 13

The Final Blow

Max disappeared the night I almost died and, once again, I was left all alone. The next few days drudged on. I lay in bed for days and never left the house, only getting up to use the bathroom.

I hadn't spoken to my family in two years or my friends in over a year and I was no longer working, so no one missed my absence. I was completely defeated in every way. I had lost the will to live. I had succumbed to the idea of this misery and torture being my life. I knew I would likely not live to see my thirtieth birthday and I was okay with that as I didn't see what life had to offer. My only comfort was weed to aid the pain, both physically and mentally.

My father was due back from his trip to France. I was worried and afraid as he also had a temper. One day, before I lived with Max, I was leaving my dad's house after we had gotten into a huge fight, which was not unusual, and Max was sitting across the road on the curb waiting for me. I was packing my bags inside when my dad got into his car and pulled a U-turn up onto the curb and Max had to jump out of the way, otherwise my father would have run right over him.

I knew my dad would be upset about the damages to the house from the party. I had been so numb to everything, I had forgotten about the shattered glass that needed repair and my father's broken trinkets.

I finally got out of bed and headed downstairs to clean up the mess. I got busy vacuuming and washing. As I cleaned, I pondered my situation. I was in a relationship with a boy who was trying to be a man, someone I no longer loved. He obviously didn't love me, no matter what he said. I had turned away my family and friends, so I had nowhere to go and no one to turn to.

I was not welcome at my mother's house. My father would be furious with me once he saw the house and he'd for sure kick us out. Max was all I had in this miserable and lonely world. Hopefully, his mother would let us move back in with her. I really didn't see any other options. I had burnt all my bridges and had no one to turn to.

I had planned to have everything organized and I would be gone by the time my father got back. I managed to get the house back in order minus some broken items. I intended on coming up with lies to explain the damages as I could not tell him the truth. As I did a final walkthrough of the house, flashbacks of the horrors that took place in each room rushed back.

If these walls could talk, what would they say? They'd seen it all. These walls now shared the horrible secrets that Max and I lived with everyday. As I walked to the front door, I stopped to take one last look at the room where we had slept, where we had made love and where I had layed for days all alone with no food and no sleep. The room was now clean—the bed made, carpet vacuumed and windows washed. The living room was spotless, ready to entertain again. There was no sign of what had occurred.

There were, of course, the holes in the glass door and the few baubles on the mantelpiece that were now broken from Max's murderous rampage that horrid night. I stood in the spot where Max had intended to end my life, where I thought I'd end it all myself, right next to the fireplace. I shuddered and hurriedly walked out the door, wondering if I'd ever set foot in this house ever again. I felt a sense of foreboding as I walked up the path to the garden gate. I said goodbye to the house and the horrors which took place inside.

I sat at the bus stop across the road staring up at the bedroom window. This house was where my parents brought me right after I was born. It was where my sister and I had been raised. It was my childhood home until it became a house of torture. I had lived in this house for most of my life. I could see a ghost-like reflection of myself staring back at me from the upstairs window with a blank, grey stare, numb to the world.

The bus dropped me off a couple of blocks away from Max's mum's house. As I walked with my suitcase dragging behind me, my thoughts wandered back to that horrible night. I honestly thought I was going to die that night and I pondered what would have happened if he had succeeded in killing me. Would my parents miss me? How long would it take people to notice I was gone? Would people blame me for my death? Would Max feel bad or happy about my death? Who would mourn for me?

I felt worthless and disgusted that this was now my life. I wondered if maybe I wasn't a good person and maybe I deserved this abuse. Maybe if I was kinder and better, I wouldn't be treated this way.

When I arrived at the house, I was feeling quite awful about myself, so I sat outside for a moment. I had to prepare myself for the acting role of the happy young couple who were very much in love. I had become quite a good actress as I had everyone fooled and no one was wise to what was happening right under their noses.

Max must have seen me sitting outside. He opened the door and gave me a hug before grabbing my suitcase and ushering me inside. He handed me some beautiful flowers and gave me a kiss on the cheek. "Dinner will be ready soon," he said. "My mum's out, so we have the house to ourselves."

"Sounds good. I'll go put my bag in the bedroom," I said, grabbing my things and heading upstairs. The bedroom was small and quite bare. A futon would be our bed. The floor was littered with Max's clothes and some dirty dishes.

The room was familiar from the days when our relationship was new. Inside these walls, our love had grown. It was sweet and innocent back then. We had spent hours there listening to music and professing our love to each other. Now it felt cold and sad as I remembered the holes in the bedroom wall. I wondered what this house would do for our relationship. I put my bag in the closet and headed back downstairs to see what was for dinner. It had been quite a while since Max had cooked, let alone shown any interest in if or when I had eaten, for that matter.

"Dinner's ready, I hope you're hungry," he said as he set a beautiful roast chicken on the table. Food would be more plentiful now that we lived with his mum. She always had a fridge full of food, as well as beer. I sat down at the table feeling a little uncomfortable as this would always be his mother's house and I had now grown accustomed to living on my own with no adults to answer to. It would take a little time getting used to not being alone anymore, but I hoped that not being alone also meant it was safer.

Dinner was chicken, potatoes and vegetables. It had been a while since we had eaten fresh vegetables, so I ate a lot, although my stomach had shrunk after months of having little food, so it didn't take long before I was full. When we were finished eating, I put our dishes in the dishwasher. "Thank you for dinner. It was really tasty. And the flowers are beautiful. I'm super tired, though, so if it's okay, I'm just going to head to bed," I said before heading up the stairs.

I had managed to find a part-time job just before we moved in. I had found a job as a trail guide on horseback.

CHAPTER 13

I had always been very passionate about horses, so I loved this job. It allowed me to be outside all day with horses and nature, on beautiful trails around a beautiful lake. On days where there were no rides, I was still able to go and ride for fun by myself. The barn was my happy place and Max didn't call to bug me so much when I was there. Summer would be coming up soon and I had planned to join a few horse shows.

I had work in the morning. Though it was still early to go to bed, staying up late was hard for me as I was emotionally drained and exhausted all the time. When I opened the bedroom door, there was a small bouquet of flowers on the bedside table. I sat on the bed and smiled. Max came into the room beaming and said, "I thought you might like a bouquet by the bed. That way, it'll be the first thing you see in the morning and the last thing you see at night."

"Thank you. They smell lovely." I answered while lying down. "I have work tomorrow," I told him. I rolled over to face the wall and grabbed the blanket. Max lay right next to me, and we fell asleep spooning. We had been apart for a week before my father was due back, so it felt nice to have arms wrapped gently around me. I had unfortunately gotten used to the feeling of being physically close to Max but also feeling alone. I felt ashamed that I even wanted his touch, but I also longed for the slightest shred of love.

Max and I had been together for three years by this point. It felt like our relationship was a small boat lost at sea with nowhere else to go. For a while, it seemed like we were just playing our parts. I was once again busy with work and even though I only worked part time, I went to the barn as often as I could. Max hung out with friends all day and since I wasn't on his case about getting a job, he was in a much better mood.

I bought our groceries. Max and I both helped out around the house and did chores for his mother in order to pay the rent. We patched the holes he had put in his bedroom wall and painted over them. We fixed the garden fence and weeded and pruned the hedges.

Things between Max and I were a little awkward for a short time. We shared little kisses and went to bed together, but we tiptoed around each other most of the time. We were keeping up appearances. To everyone else, our relationship was healthy and loving. But there was something dark and immensely powerful between us: the secret that we shared.

Occasionally, I would still join Max when he visited his older lady friend at the cheap housing complex. I had

CHAPTER 13

grown rather close to Max's friend's daughters and they loved when I visited. Their mum and Max locked themselves in the room to smoke and I watched a movie with the girls.

We would still go downtown and visit Max's friend who worked at the mall. Rick lived not too far from Max's mum's house, but he was never home; he was always working. Rick was always working as he supported his mother and he was never able to come out with us after work to hang out. He was a longtime friend of Max's and the boys had introduced me to smoking marijuana. Rick had epilepsy and the marijuana kept his seizures at bay. I had never seen him have a seizure myself, so I figured the weed worked. We would go visit him at his job and wait for him to have a lunch break, and then, we'd all go outside and smoke.

Rick was a really nice guy and he and I hit it off right away. He was gay and he was always complimenting my clothes. Sometimes, he joined us in the mall to go shopping and he picked out some awesome earrings for me. He was a fun-loving guy and always happy and smiling and I loved his sarcastic humour. Max and I always enjoyed hanging out with him. He always kept things light and fun.

One day, we went downtown later in the afternoon as we knew Rick would be off work. Max and I were both determined to get Rick to come and hang out with us after his shift. We managed to convince him to come out with us, so when he got off work at 7 p.m., we all went to a liquor store and bought a few bottles of Growers Cider. Rick had stolen a few cups from his workplace, so we all drank some right away. Max and Rick chugged a 2-liter bottle. I could not chug alcohol, nor did I want to. The boys got drunk real fast. I enjoyed a milder buzz.

We went for a walk through the downtown area carrying liquor in my purse and in Rick's backpack. We walked along the beach and sat for a short while to split a joint. We walked through the park and once it got late, we headed home. Rick lived close to Max, so when we got off the bus, we all hung out at the bus stop and smoked another joint. I was sober by that point and Rick was beginning to sober up himself. Max, however, had drunk the last 2-liter on his own, so he was completely wasted.

By then, it was roughly 2 o'clock in the morning. I was exhausted and ready to call it a night. Max, however, was not. We began arguing as I wanted to go home and he wanted me to stay. I had told him that he could stay with Rick and continue to hang out, but he wanted me there as well.

CHAPTER 13

He argued that Rick now liked me better than him because we went shopping together and because I had gone to visit Rick a couple of times without him. Max grew upset and began arguing with both Rick and I.

I decided to start walking up the hill heading home and Max completely lost it. He started yelling and ran up the pedestrian overpass. He climbed the railing so that he was hanging over the road and oncoming traffic. Luckily, it was after 2 o'clock in the morning, so there was little traffic, although it was a major roadway and would be full of morning commuters in just a few hours. Max was screaming at us and threatening to jump off the overpass. His friend Rick was much more relaxed than I was.

"C'mon man. Come down from there and relax. Come smoke a joint with me," he said calmly.

"Max, get down from there! This isn't funny. You're going to hurt yourself," I frantically yelled, "You're going to kill yourself!" After a few minutes, he began to find this amusing.

"I bet I could land it. How much are you guys willing to bet?" he yelled back in a cocky manner. He took one leg and dangled it over the road below him. Then, he took one hand off the railing. Half his body was now over the road, barely holding onto the railing. I was terrified.

"Max, what are you doing? Get down from there! This isn't funny," I screamed. I looked for Rick, who was starting to make his way up the overpass and slowly towards Max. I couldn't hear what the boys were saying to each other but after a couple of minutes, Rick managed to convince Max to come back over the railing. Once he was back on the safe side of the railing, I felt myself let out a sigh of relief.

The boys eventually came down the overpass. Rick's arm was around Max's shoulder and they were laughing. We all then headed towards the house. Rick decided that he would crash on the couch as it would allow me to go to sleep since he could entertain Max.

Max was sick and twisted. He would act out just to get a rise out of people. He liked making people, especially me, uncomfortable.

One day, I was lying in bed watching TV and Max walked in. He sat down on the bed and started telling me about some old friends of his. "A friend of mine who used to live in the townhome complex, she moved away a few years ago and she'll be in town. I haven't seen her in years. She will stay here with us as my mum and sister will be away for the weekend, so there's plenty of room. She's bringing her girlfriend, too."

"Okay, well, I work this weekend, so I'll only really be

CHAPTER 13

around in the evenings," I replied. I didn't care much to hang out with Max and his friends as much as I had already done. The only thing they ever did was drink and smoke weed all the time. It was getting boring for me. Now that I was working again, I had started to put money aside. My new focus these days was to save and hopefully be able to live on my own.

I was never comfortable living in Max's mother's house. She was nice enough, but she drank every weekend and she'd come home drunk. I worked most weekends, so it was difficult to sleep in this environment. I also just missed having a place that I could walk around in my underwear if I wanted to and not have to worry about other people. Max was rarely home either. He spent all his time at a friend's house just down the road and sometimes he spent the night there. We didn't see each other very often.

Maybe a week after he told me of his friends' visit, they showed up. Max was super excited to have his old friend back. He had told me they were close when they were younger and that they were always running around together causing mischief. "This is Jess," he said after hurriedly opening the door and giving her a hug. I introduced myself.

"Hi. This is my girlfriend, Amanda," she said, wrapping her arm around her girlfriend's shoulder. It was evening, so while Max helped them get settled in his sister's room, I cooked dinner. It was a late night of beers and catching up. The girls were genuinely nice, but I headed upstairs pretty early as I had to work in the morning. We all agreed we would hang out the following night, order pizza and then go out.

My workday went quickly. I took some people out on a trail ride and then rode my favourite horse for fun. I had started jumping him and he was so good at it. I loved my time with him. We shared a strong bond. I was so happy whenever I was at the barn.

Max spent the day with the girls downtown visiting old hangout spots and other friends. I was looking forward to hanging out with Jess and Amanda since we got along really well. It also helped that Max was in such a good mood with his friend around. It almost felt like the beginning of our relationship when we enjoyed each other's company and hanging out, before all the stress and the violence.

When I got home, they had already begun to drink and were ready to go out. I quickly hopped in the shower. I was excited and a little nervous as I hadn't been out in a long time. I also didn't have any bruises to cover for the first time in a while, so I decided to wear a dress and do my makeup. They had ordered pizza so we could eat and pre-game before heading out. Going out was expensive, so it was better to eat and drink before leaving.

Max's mother had a stash of alcohol that included beer, vodka and tequila in a cupboard above the fridge. Max grabbed the vodka and gave us shots. He made me a vodka and cranberry cocktail as I had still not acquired a taste for beer. Once the pizza was gone and we had all had several shots, we headed to the bus stop to go downtown. Jess pulled out a joint as we walked. We all shared the joint and chatted.

It was a Saturday night, so the bus was full. There were lots of young people just like us headed downtown for a night of fun. Drunk people love to strike up conversations with strangers and one started chatting with me. He was asking me where we were going to party and Max told me to switch spots with him so I was seated between the window and him. He was protective of me and didn't like me talking to other guys. I think he thought the guy was hitting on me since I was wearing a dress.

When we arrived downtown, we went into a bar and ordered a pitcher to share. I ordered my own drink as I didn't want beer. The server checked our IDs and that was when we discovered that Amanda wasn't of legal age yet, so the waitress informed us she couldn't serve any of us. We were all a little upset, but there wasn't anything we could do. Max and Jess quickly chugged the pitcher of beer before the waitress could take it away and then we all got up and ran out of the bar. We headed towards a liquor store.

The girls and Max bought a bunch of beers and some vodka and pop to chase it down with. I bought a 6-pack of Vector (a very sweet and quite delicious vodka and juice drink). We walked until we found a bench in a small square next to a church. Max called one of his friends to come join us and not long after, there were quite a few of us drinking in the park.

It was a warm night. Everyone was in a good mood. When it got dark after a couple of hours, we walked towards the bus stop but decided to stop at the inner harbor and sit for a little while. Max and I used to love going down by the water and listening to the waves and see the boats decorated with their little lights. It was quite beautiful in the moonlight and very peaceful.

We sat for probably another hour. Then, noticing the time, we quickly went to the bus stop. We were lucky we got there thirty minutes ahead of the last bus of the night. There were a few other stragglers with us waiting for the bus. By the time it arrived, it was very late and getting chilly.

CHAPTER 13

I fell asleep on the bus. I was woken up by a slap on my bare leg. "Wake up. Our stop is next," Max said. The thought of having to walk another twenty minutes up a hill in heels tormented me. I had even dreaded this walk in running shoes. Now, I was exhausted and inebriated and my feet hurt from walking all evening. The girls laughed at me with sympathy as I removed my shoes and began to walk towards home barefoot. Jess had never worn heels, so she didn't know the pain, but Amanda said she did.

When we arrived home, all the lights were off. Max had to search for the house key because he never carried it on him; his mother wouldn't let him since he would always lose it. When he finally found it under a plant pot, he opened the door and I headed straight for the couch.

Amanda and I were already sober by that point and Jess and Max were starting to sober up as they had drunk a lot more than we had. I was cold and my feet were so sore, I fell on the couch and covered myself in a blanket. We all sat around the living room and chatted for a short time.

"I'm going to call it a night. I'm exhausted and I've got to work tomorrow. Good night," I announced as I went around giving hugs. I then headed upstairs for a quick shower. Once I was clean and warm in my pajamas, I lay in bed to sleep. After maybe an hour or so Max came into the room.

"Can you sleep on the floor? I need to stretch out and I don't want you to climb over me in the morning when you have to head out," Max said exhaustedly. "Are you kidding me?" I asked, shocked, "I'm the one who has to wake up to go to work. I need a good night's sleep. I'll sleep on your side of the bed, which is closer to the door, and you can sleep on mine and then I won't wake you when I get up. How does that sound?"

"No! Go sleep downstairs then," he answered, beginning to get angry.

"The girls are down there chatting. Why don't you go sleep downstairs? I'm already comfy and ready for bed," I answered him calmly. This argument continued for a short time and then he angrily changed his clothes. I rolled away from him to face the wall. I was curled up and trying to sleep when I felt him sit heavily on the bed and lie down. All of a sudden, I felt a sharp pain on the side of my face and eye. Then, everything went black.

When I awoke, I heard yelling and screaming from Jess and Amanda. Amanda was hovering over me and asking me if I was alright. I had no idea what had happened, but I could have guessed. Jess moved the bed away from the wall and helped me up from the floor. I had rolled off the side of the bed and become wedged between the bed and the wall after Max elbowed me in the face. The girls were in a panic as Amanda took me downstairs and Jess was yelling at Max.

"Has this happened before?" Amanda asked me very gently. I nodded. My head was throbbing, and I couldn't look anywhere other than my feet. Everything was fuzzy. "Does this happen often?" she asked, scooting closer to me on the couch and putting her arm around me. Again, I nodded.

"Don't worry. We'll get you out of here. Will you come with us if we find somewhere to go for the night?" she asked a bit more determinedly. I looked up at her and nodded. Jess came downstairs and she was obviously very upset. She began asking me the same questions that Amanda had asked me and Amanda kindly answered them for me. She came and sat next to me on the couch as well. I began to cry.

The secret that I had been living with was finally out and there was no way we could pretend anymore. I felt relieved knowing that I didn't have to live a lie anymore.

I heard Max coming down the stairs. He came into the living room and as soon as he looked at me, Jess stepped in front of him. "Stop! Do not go near Joy. You stay away from her. She told us this is not the first time. I can't believe this. You are one of my closest friends. How could you do this?

We aren't spending the night here anymore," she said with hurt and disbelief in her voice.

Max replied with excuses, but she wasn't hearing any of it. She was disgusted by this side of her friend she had never seen. He tried apologizing and saying he was tired, that it was late. He told me he loved me, and he wanted to go to bed and pretend as if none of the night's events had happened.

When he didn't get his way with attempting niceties, he changed his tactic and turned mean. He started yelling at us all. Swearing and spitting, he was so angry. He was angry because for once it wasn't just him against me all by myself. I had backup this time and because they had seen it, the lies could not be bought and excuses were just that: excuses.

"Fuck all of you!" he said as he headed towards the kitchen. Right away, I grew nervous. Max, angry and in the kitchen was never a safe bet.

"Girls," I said anxiously standing up, "He's going to come back in here with a knife. This isn't good. He's thrown knives at me a few times now. We should all be careful and leave." I moved close to the sliding door nearby since the front door was through the kitchen. The girls looked at me in shock and stepped back with me. Max came back into the living room. "Max, put that down," I said with my voice wavering.

"You think I'm just a fucked up monster," he shouted at me with disgust, waving a knife at us.

There are three of us against one of him. What is he thinking? Is he going to hurt all three of us?

He yelled horrible things and started name calling. He was upset that his friend was not taking his side. He felt betrayed. "I'll show you how fucked up I am." He quickly drew the knife up and stuck out his arm in front of him, palm up. "This'll show you how much I care about you." Before we knew it, he cut a chunk of skin out of his upper forearm and held it in front of him. He waved it at us with a horribly disturbing smirk on his face, and blood dripping down his arm. He then threw it at me and it hit my chest.

I felt like the wind had been taken out of my sails. I felt completely and utterly defeated. My knees buckled and I crashed to the floor. Amanda knelt by me, cradling me as Jess ran to Max. He was now sitting in a chair and Jess was finding something to stop the blood as it was covering his arm and dripping onto the floor. She was contemplating calling an ambulance as no one could drive nor did we even have a vehicle.

Once again, Max had manipulated the situation so he was the one being cared for. I was absolutely horrified by how truly sick he was.

CHAPTER 14

Escape

The morning after the incident, I awoke in Amber's room. We couldn't find anywhere to go the night before and Jess was worried about leaving Max as he had bled a lot. I had locked myself in Amber's room and fallen asleep. I was scheduled to work, but my head was throbbing and I had an obvious bump. I called into work and told my boss I was sick and unable to work.

Jess and Amanda woke up soon after I did and came to check on me. We all started packing our bags. Jess and Amanda meant to stay a few more days, but Jess had decided she didn't want to stick around, so they booked an early flight home. We all carried our bags to the bus stop and got off the bus downtown. The bus ride felt long and we were all silent. Jess and Amanda hoped on another bus that would take them to the airport and I wandered around, hoping to find a friend with a couch to sleep on.

I moved out of Max's mum's house and felt very disoriented. I hadn't spoken to my parents or my sister in two years. I had lost most of my friends and I had distanced myself from Max's. I hadn't been to school in over a year. I was a wreck with my emotions. I didn't know how to handle myself or who I had become. After many nights of sleeping on anyone's couch who would let me, I finally mustered up the courage to phone my mum.

She was happy to hear that Max and I had broken up and let me move back into my old bedroom. Of course, I didn't give her details about the relationship or the break-up, but I think she knew it had not been good. She put me under strict house rules: no drinking or drugs and I had to go back to school. I was more than happy to oblige as I would be safe and fed.

After receiving both apologetic and threatening phone calls from Max, I changed my cell phone number and blocked him just in case. I also blocked him on social media. I went to the cell phone company and cancelled the contract for Max's phone as it was under my name. Unfortunately, he had racked up his bill to $300 dollars, which I had to pay. He sent me emails saying how much he missed me and loved me and how he couldn't live without me. He threatened to kill himself by deliberately overdosing on cocaine if I didn't go back to him.

I ignored every email and made sure to never be downtown as I didn't want to bump into him or any of his friends. I even changed my time slot for school so as not to see him. After a month or so of being ignored, he became furious and once again changed his tactic. He began sending me emails telling me I was a piece of shit. He threatened to kill me and told me that if he couldn't have me that no one else could. He told me I wasn't loveable and all sorts of mean and hurtful things. But I never responded. He sent me those horrible emails for probably two or three months. Finally, they ended.

It took me a long time to comfortably talk about what had happened. I had never told anyone and the only people who knew were Amanda and Jess, only because they had witnessed it. When I turned nineteen, I never went out to party as Max was a few months younger than I was and he wouldn't allow me to go. He convinced me it wasn't safe for a girl to go out by herself. So, when I was finally free of him for my twentieth birthday, I went out clubbing.

I loved being out on my own and not having to worry about getting home to Max or even having to think about how I was behaving. I had so much fun when I went clubbing and the people there were generally very happy and friendly. I would get dressed up and feel beautiful and sexy. I hadn't felt good about myself in a long time. Guys would buy me drinks and we'd dance all night. It made me feel free. I loved the numbing happy feeling that came with alcohol consumption.

I enjoyed it so much, I became a regular at one particular club downtown and was there at least three nights a week. Then occasionally, I'd try a few other places with people I'd met. I bumped into one of my old high school friends one night while I was out and she was with some of her friends. We decided to party together and had a blast. We decided from then on to go out together more regularly and I'd often spend the night at her place. We would get super drunk and dance until four in the morning.

After maybe six months or so, I felt more comfortable hanging out downtown. I had made new friends who assured me they could take care of Max if he decided to show himself. My new friends were like me. Many had been through some tough situations. A few of them were homeless. We were all just lost souls struggling with our

CHAPTER 14

own demons. We would hang around and smoke weed or drink. A few were underage, but they all knew people who would buy them alcohol. I would buy some for myself and then we'd all meet up and go sit in a park or by the ocean and we'd drink.

I was having fun, but at the same time, anyone who knew me well would have known that I was hurting. I didn't trust anyone. I felt like I didn't know how to act around people anymore. I had been living a lie, a double life, for so long. I didn't know who I was anymore, and I didn't know how to emotionally deal with this big secret I'd been hiding. I drank to make myself feel better and to wash away my misery. The truth is that the pain is only temporarily forgotten when you're absolutely shit-faced. The next morning, the hurt floods in, so you have to start drinking again.

I felt so lost. I was partying every night with anyone I could find who wanted to party. I made my own friends out partying, but as you can imagine, they weren't real friends because they didn't know me, and I didn't know them. They were just available to party.

Although I was enjoying myself, I never let my guard down. I was always anxiety-ridden with the fear of bumping into Max or any of his friends. I only hung out in areas where I knew Max was unlikely to be. I never went to the mall to visit his friend Rick who I had really enjoyed hanging out with.

The first time I ever opened up about what happened, I was drunk. A few friends were having a bonfire on the beach and I decided to go. It was a lot of fun. It was a nice, warm night and everyone brought their own alcohol. My friend Jon came with me. I was pretty wasted. I had to pee, but since we were on the beach, there was no bathroom or outhouse. I asked Jon to come with me and stand guard while I peed in a bush.

He sat on a log watching the ocean as I stumbled around looking for a hidden spot. Afterwards, I joined him on the log and we chatted. I don't remember how it came about, but I think Jon asked me what had been going on with me and brought up the horrible New Year's Eve party. Once I started opening up, I completely fell apart. I told him that Max had been abusive for the last couple of years of our relationship. I told him about Max putting knives to my throat and choking me. Jon was very upset and sad that I didn't feel safe enough to confide in him earlier, when it was happening. I told him it wasn't his fault and that there was nothing he could have done. I cried on his shoulder while he wrapped his arms around me and held me tightly.

CHAPTER 14

I felt safe for the first time in a long time. When we joined the party again, he stayed close to me, protecting me as his friend.

When I opened up to my mother, I had come home from a night of partying and I was still a little drunk. I had brought a 6-pack of my favourite vodka drinks home. My mum had stayed up waiting for me to get home safe, although she never admitted that that was what she was doing.

She was on the couch, and I sat on the other couch facing her. I opened a bottle and asked her if she wanted some. She flatly said no and I drank the whole bottle, chugging it down. She asked me what had happened between Max and I and how the relationship had ended. She mentioned how I had changed a lot in the three years I had been with Max. I slowly and somewhat nervously opened up to her.

I told her that Max had been physically abusive towards me for the past couple of years. She told me that she had suspected something like that as my behaviour had been completely out of character for me. She hugged me and comforted me.

She forgave me for my behaviour and our relationship moved forward and was greatly improved. She didn't agree with my partying all the time, but she understood that I was mentally in turmoil and she respected that I had to figure things out for myself.

I went to visit my sister one day. She had moved in with her boyfriend. We sat on the couch and I cried in her arms as I told her about Max and some small details. She held me tightly until my tears eventually stopped. She asked me why I didn't leave. I didn't know how to answer her. I had tried to get rid of him many times, but he always came back. It hadn't been easy.

I reached out to my old best friend from high school. She had turned her back on me and it hurt me badly. I wanted to know why she had abandoned me. I told her about Max but gave no specific details. She apologized for not being there for me, but she had known that something was not right and when I made it clear that I wasn't leaving Max, she didn't want to watch someone she cared about be hurt.

One day, I got a phone call from one of Max's friends. He told me I had to stop spreading lies and bad-mouthing Max. I didn't know what he had heard or from whom. He threatened to shut me up if I didn't stop. I was upset and slightly scared, but I told him that he had no idea what happened behind closed doors and that maybe his friend Max wasn't as nice as he thought.

CHAPTER 14

I waited almost a year before telling my father. I felt a lot of guilt for the lies that I had told him, the fact that I never paid him rent while Max and I had lived in the upstairs suite, the fact that Max had done quite a bit of damage to the walls and about the party that I had thrown while he was away. I hadn't really spoken with him since then and I was afraid to face him. I met him at a Chinese restaurant that was ten minutes away from my mum's house.

I had my mother drive me as I didn't have a driver's license or a vehicle. I asked her to stay close, assuming my visit with my father would end promptly and angrily. My father and I sat down, and he, of course, brought up how irresponsible I was and how I never stayed in touch with him. I didn't know how to go about telling him what had happened.

I started by telling him how I had lost my job and couldn't afford rent. When he asked me why I was fired I told him that Max had become violent and I had been late for work a few times, and that my demeanour had changed and I wasn't pleasant to be around. He had a hard time believing what I was telling him, so I gave him more and more details while reading his face. I knew I'd have to be more specific in order to get the message across.

I began by telling him that Max had begun to throw items at me, such as the TV. I told him that Max had hit me. I told him about Max threatening me with knives. He had an extremely hard time swallowing all the information and just didn't seem to take in any of it. He told me that maybe it wasn't as bad as I thought since women tended to exaggerate and wanted to be seen as victims. He told me he would have suspected something if it had been violent. He had heard us arguing but nothing more. I told him that he never saw it because I didn't want him to. I hid the scars with makeup and extra layers.

My dad chose to ignore what I was telling him and instead of acknowledging it, he focused on the subject of the New Year's party and became upset about the damage that had been done to the house. He was yelling at me in the restaurant and people started staring. I didn't know how to answer his questions about the damages done and how they had happened. I became very uncomfortable and decided to leave.

My mum came and took me home. I cried the whole drive home. I was very disheartened that my father just didn't want to listen to me as I attempted to open up. My own father didn't believe me, and he was more concerned with the events at the party than the fact that I had been horribly treated and badly hurt physically as well as mentally and emotionally. I decided to keep silent and not tell anyone else about what had happened. After so long of holding in this secret, to be faced with skepticism was extremely damaging.

I felt like the only place I wasn't judged, and where people could relate with my pain, was on the street with those other troubled and lost souls. However, after almost a year, my mother had grown tired of my partying and late hours. My night life was what made my day-to-day life bearable, but I was now under my mother's roof, so things became exceedingly difficult for us. She didn't trust me. I was not acting the way I used to, and she thought that I was doing drugs on top of it. I wasn't and I told her as much, but she didn't believe me. She once had me strip naked to prove I wasn't trying to smuggle drugs into the house. This hurt me deeply. I was humiliated.

I began dating a guy named Nic who I partied with. I had met him when I was still with Max as he had been a new student at school. He also knew the street kids I had met and befriended.

Nic was a nice guy and would buy me drinks often. He was six foot three and 250 pounds. He looked tough, but he was a total teddy bear. I think subconsciously I chose him because I felt safe with him. I had told him a little about Max and he hated woman beaters.

We dated for a few years. I never forgot our first fight. He was upset about something and when he raised his voice, I flinched. I was so used to being hit during arguments that I just assumed it was coming. When I opened my eyes, I could see the sadness in his eyes. He then took me in his arms and told me that he would never hit me. He never did.

It was then, when I was sober, that I began to really notice the effects of an abusive relationship. I would flinch whenever any man would raise a hand around me. Even if it was just for a hug or a high five, I would be terrified and recoil. One time, Nic was tickling me on his bed. The bed was detached from the wall and I fell between the bed frame and the wall. I screamed, terrified, as it brought me flashbacks of the last time I had blacked out when Max elbowed me in the face. It was terrifying and once I realized I wasn't in danger, that I wasn't with Max anymore, I sobbed uncontrollably. The poor guy didn't know what to do, so he didn't touch me and gently coaxed me out with soft, kind words.

Since living with my mum, I had started going back to school. Most of my old friends were still there and it was great to see them again. Some of them would join me downtown and we'd hang out. One time, a few of us were smoking weed and I had a terrible experience. I was hallucinating and in my vision, I saw fists coming out of nowhere trying to punch me in the face. I leaned back to try to avoid them, jerking my neck. The fists were endless and as I dodged one punch, another came, and another, and another. I eventually gave myself whiplash and ended up on the floor as I had been leaning further and further back. I didn't smoke weed for a long time after that.

After being with Max, I became super aware of my own personal bubble—and if anyone was in my bubble, especially men. Whenever I was in public, I did not feel comfortable or safe if there was a man standing directly behind me and I couldn't really see him. This was very difficult and stressful for me as I constantly took the public bus, which was often very busy. If I suspected a man was behind me, I would shift in my seat so that instead of being behind me where I couldn't see, I would be able to see him either beside me or in front of me. I would also just switch seats altogether if there was a man seated behind me and I couldn't shift in my seat. Often when the bus was crowded, I would stand with my back to a wall, facing everyone. As the years went by, this was one thing that stuck with me. Unfortunately, it didn't matter who this man was—my father, a friend, a stranger—I did not feel safe with a man behind me.

After a year and a half of partying and dating a new guy, Max came back into my life. I hadn't heard from him since the horrible emails but one day, there he was again in my inbox. He had sent me an email apologizing for everything that had happened. He told me he had thought a lot about me over the last year and had many regrets. He told me he still cared for me and asked me to give him a chance to treat me the way I deserved to be treated.

Things at home were not going well for me at this time. My mother had grown quite upset with my partying. I hadn't spoken to my father since the restaurant and I'd recently broken up with Nic. So, I decided I would go.

Max said he would pay for me to bus up north and for a return ticket. He had a place to stay where there was room for me. He promised me that if the visit didn't go well, he'd pay the extra money to change return dates. He sent me my tickets by email, and I was to leave in a few days. I didn't want to admit to anyone that I was going to see Max, so I told my mother and friends that I was going up north with a friend to visit a horse ranch. I had become such a good liar that everyone believed me.

I was nervous when I boarded the Greyhound bus. I didn't really know why I had decided to go, but I figured I'd at least get closure. When I arrived, Max was waiting for me. It was slightly awkward seeing him again. I didn't know if he was going to want to hug or kiss me but luckily, he didn't force anything. He just smiled and said "Hi." He seemed to have changed. He was happy, and he discussed his new job at a bar that he genuinely enjoyed. When we arrived at his house, I was rather underwhelmed. It was a tiny room, like a garden shed, with a fridge, a bed, and a microwave. That first night, it was very strange to once again be lying next to Max. I never imagined I would be back there.

During the days, he worked, so I occupied myself by reading and going for walks. There were a few days where a friend and coworker of Max's would keep me company on his days off. Most nights, I'd walk to the bar just before Max's shift ended and we ate dinner there and hung out with his coworkers. It was a tiny town and there was nothing to do there.

I was alone a lot, however, and it gave me time to think. Though he had treated me much better and never physically hurt me this time, I had caught him messaging a female coworker of his. They clearly had an attraction between them, and I wasn't about to get caught up in that. After two weeks, I left and Max wanted me to return to him. I told him I would consider it, but I had already made up my mind. I had moved on and no longer had feelings for him.

When I returned home, life resumed as normal. I continued to go to school and party at night. However, I felt like I now had closure and I could close the chapter on Max. I had my own emotional scars to tend to.

EPILOGUE

Looking back now, it all seems like a bad dream. It was so long ago. I have spent years going to therapy, getting the help I needed in order to overcome what I endured and move forward with my life. One of the hardest lessons was learning to recognize the signs of abuse in new relationships so as not to end up in another toxic or abusive relationship.

Three years ago, I was discussing relationships with a friend and it made me more aware of how often people find themselves in unhealthy and toxic relationships. I hope my book reaches those who might wonder if their partners' behaviour is toxic. It isn't always black and white. Sometimes, it can be hard to know where to draw the line. My wish for this book is to be a shining light for those who are struggling to leave a dangerous situation.

There is an uncomfortable air around those who simply did not want to hear about others' struggles in their relationships. I became aware of so many women like myself who doubted their own stories and did not speak up for themselves. They were lost and alone as I had once been. My heart went out to them as I could understand their struggle. I began to enjoy sharing stories of my experience because I knew my story had the power to help other women. I especially wanted to help other young girls who may be awkward and shy and easy for an abuser to target.

My abuser got away with his actions. I was so terrified of him, I just wanted him out of my life. After a few years, when I finally became angry with what had transpired, it was too late to do anything about it. Unfortunately, this is why abusers often get away with their crimes. Sadly, I found out that Max went on to abuse another girlfriend he had after me. This book is a warning to the abusers out there: We are not victims; we are survivors. We are strong and we are brave. You may think we are weak, but watch out. When we come into our own, we will fight and we will win.

I hope this book can also be a guide for those who know someone in an abusive relationship. I decided to write my story in hopes of helping families and friends of victims understand what it is actually like to be in an abusive relationship so that they can possibly better help someone they love who is in one. The first step would be to have compassion and understanding. When a person leaves a toxic relationship, they feel like a failure. They feel shame. They want to hide their head in the sand.

One thing I didn't know until recently was that abusers also have self-esteem issues. Though Max had a monster inside of him, when he wasn't yelling at me or beating me up, he would repeatedly tell me he loved me. He would tell me that we belonged together and that he would die if I left him, that he would kill himself if I ever left. He told me that leaving him would be like me leaving him to rot and die. He would tell me how much he needed me.

It was always when he had the lost pathetic eyes that I just wanted to make him feel better and let him know I loved him and that I would never leave him. I couldn't do that. Not to someone I loved and who clearly needed me. I thought he loved me but just had an odd and unhealthy way of showing it.

Some women, like myself, have a somewhat unhealthy, maternal side to them that believes that love can heal all. You think if you love someone enough, they will quit drinking, smoking, doing drugs or even beating you. Unfortunately, it doesn't work that way. I learnt you can't change someone who doesn't want to change. They can fake it and pretend; they can hide the truth, but they don't change.

I learnt in my relationship with Max that love doesn't solve everything. It takes more than love to make a relationship work and both parties must be in love to make it work. The most important thing is respect for each other as well as for yourself. If someone wants to change, they will. Max didn't want to change, and it took me a long time to learn and, most of all, accept that.

Learning how to recognize what real love looks like is still ongoing for me. Another big lesson was acknowledging that I deserve to be loved and happy. I learned that I deserve to be in a healthy relationship and that it is okay to stand up for myself and demand respect. I also learnt a lot about myself, what I liked and what I was able to do. I had spent years letting Max make all the decisions and plans that I didn't really know what I enjoyed doing in my spare time. I discovered that I love to read and write. I went to California for several months to visit an old friend of mine

I hadn't seen in years. I was finally able to discover life on my own terms and discover myself. I found out that I am a kind person and a dreamer with ambition and passion.

I got a job and was able to keep it and be happy. With my job, I realized how much money I could save without a deadbeat boyfriend sucking me dry. I was able to go out for dinner with friends. I picked up riding lessons as it was something I had always wanted to do and something I was very passionate about. I also began to spend more time around horses in general. At the age of twenty-one, I was fortunate enough to be able to join my father when he went to France. I took a horse training course as I wanted to help abused and neglected horses. I felt connected to some of the previously abused horses I had begun to work with as I felt we had that in common. When I was twenty-three, I attended college and got a degree to be a Veterinary Assistant. It had been a dream of mine for several years and I was able to get a job in a veterinary clinic.

Today I feel very strong and very proud of the woman I have become. I know myself and my worth. I hope to empower others so they may know that there is light at the end of the tunnel.

You have power and you deserve to be loved.

RED FLAGS

A red flag is a behaviour that a spouse, partner, boyfriend or girlfriend may show that are warnings of an unhealthy relationship. If you recognize one or more of these red flags in your relationship, you may be in a toxic relationship. These are all red flags to watch out for in your partner.

1. They constantly need to know where you are and what you are doing. Contacting you multiple times every day. It's more than them checking on you if you aren't feeling well.

2. They begin to isolate you. They take all your time, and little is left for your family, friends or yourself. Max wouldn't let me hang out with my friends unless he was there and when I had made plans with my friends, he would always insist I spend the time with him instead.
3. They cause a rift between you and someone close to you. If there is already a rift, they make it bigger. For example, I wasn't getting along with my mother, so Max would add to the tension and stress by saying mean things about her.
4. They have severe anger issues and take it out on walls, doors, etc.
5. They play mind games with you. One minute they make you feel loved and important and the next, they are calling you names, yelling at you, being disrespectful.
6. Gaslighting: they manipulate you into thinking that you are making up scenarios or how bad the situation is.
7. They blame you for everything that is wrong with the relationship. They are always right.
8. They make all the decisions in your relationship and never ask you how you feel or what you want.

9. They make you quit a job or something you enjoy in life; for example, art classes or swimming.
10. They have hurt you in any physical way: hitting, punching, kicking, slapping, etc.
11. Any form of mental, physical and emotional abuse should be considered a red flag.

Manufactured by Amazon.ca
Bolton, ON

25948177R00134